The Heart of Valor

by

Connie Y Harris

Men and Women of Valor

Copyright Notice
This is a work of fiction. Names, characters, places, and incidents are either the product of the author's imagination or are used fictitiously, and any resemblance to actual persons living or dead, business establishments, events, or locales, is entirely coincidental.

The Heart of Valor

COPYRIGHT © 2025 by Connie Y Harris

All rights reserved. No part of this book may be used or reproduced in any manner whatsoever including the purpose of training artificial intelligence technologies in accordance with Article 4(3) of the Digital Single Market Directive 2019/790, The Wild Rose Press expressly reserves this work from the text and data mining exception. Only brief quotations embodied in critical articles or reviews may be allowed.
Contact Information: info@thewildrosepress.com

Cover Art by *Lisa Dawn MacDonald*

The Wild Rose Press, Inc.
PO Box 708
Adams Basin, NY 14410-0708
Visit us at www.thewildrosepress.com

Publishing History
First Edition, 2025
Trade Paperback ISBN 978-1-5092-6269-4
Digital ISBN 978-1-5092-6270-0

Men and Women of Valor
Published in the United States of America

Dedication

To my readers, thank you. Your support energizes me and sparks my creative energy.

My best memories as a teenager come from my summers spent at Fort Benning, Georgia. Although young, the dedicated resolve of the soldiers training for war made an indelible impression on me. I'm convinced they were then and are now steadfast in their resolve to defend our shores. Whether in an airport, train station or at a coffee shop, thank them for their service.

Special acknowledge to my great-niece and a U.S. Marine, Kacie Songorov. Beautiful, brave and a true patriot. You go girl!

Chapter One

Kacie O'Shea grabbed the box cutter and exposed the blade. With her legs braced in a wide stance, she waved the utility knife in a circular motion as if it were a magic wand. "Which one of you wants to get cut first?"

The boxes which filled the living room remained unopened. The move from the popular tourist city of Oceanside, Southern California to the small town of Winding Creek, Colorado, was a welcome but one-hundred-and-eighty-degree change. Which box held her hoodies? She glanced out the window at the shimmering leaves of the Aspens, the quintessential Colorado tree, with its deep reds and glowing shades of gold.

A long way from Camp Pendleton and her former home as a sergeant in the Marines, she retained many of the values the Corps taught her with discipline at the top of the list. *I better get started. The new job starts at 08:00 on Monday.* Always motivated by challenge, she set the timer on her tactical GPS watch, a parting gift from her MP unit, and with strategic precision weaved in and out of the boxes, slicing the packing tape off each top.

A quick double knock at her front door stopped her in her tracks. Only one person announced their arrival with that signature tap. Her old boss, First Sergeant

Davy Crockett, real name Mark Davis Crockett, stood on her doorstep with a bottle of her favorite tequila and a huge, weathered smile. She closed the blade and tucked it into her cargo pants, then embraced his wide chest with both arms before stepping back to 'pretend punch' him. He successfully blocked her, as usual, but this was their dance. They laughed in unison as she waved him into her new house.

"Nice digs," he said with his head on a swivel as he surveyed the room.

"Nice try," she retorted, snatching the bottle out of his hand. "Let's have a drink and get caught up. Then we can do some buzzed unboxing."

"Glad to help." He followed her into the kitchen and slid onto a stool at the counter. "How are things?"

She understood he meant how are you managing your PTSD? You know *the* thing that caused your early retirement from what you thought would be a lifetime of serving.

"The change of environment was a good decision." She frowned. "Tell me you didn't come all the way here to ask me that?"

"I had extended leave time and decided a road trip would be fun. Besides, my sister lives in Denver."

"You're a terrible liar," she huffed. "I own a phone and have you on speed dial First Sergeant." Kacie opened the cabinet and removed two shot glasses along with a shaker of cinnamon. When she placed them on the counter, they connected with a loud crack. Noticing his puzzled expression, she added, "I learned a new and tasty way to enjoy our little Mexican agave plant."

While Crockett looked on, Kacie retrieved two navel oranges from a glass bowl on the counter and tossed one to him. "Peel, please."

Dutifully, he peeled the orange and with a questioning glance began to separate the pieces.

"You catch on fast, Mr. Crockett," she teased. "Are you going to make me get you drunk to find out why the surprise visit?" She finished peeling her orange, laid it next to his and propped both elbows on the counter. "I'm ready." She raised her eyebrows and gave him her brightest smile.

"Okay, okay." He drummed his fingers on the marble countertop. "You have your first assignment coming up and I wanted to make sure you're squared away. I do plan to visit my sister."

"You recommended me for this job to the owner and your combat brother, Vince Samuels." She poured the liquid gold into each shot glass. "Watch and learn."

Kacie shook a line of cinnamon on the ridge edge of her hand and licked it, tilted her head back and threw the tequila down her throat. Then one-handed, grabbed an orange slice and sucked its juice. "Ahh." She licked her lips. "Your turn."

Mark Davis Crockett followed Kacie's example and emptied the contents of his glass into his mouth, swished, then swallowed. "That's pretty good."

"Do you know what the assignment is? All squared away. No night terrors, hands not shaking, and had the tightest shot grouping at the gun range yesterday."

"I'm impressed but not surprised."

"Nothing definite yet." She gazed at him with a swinish suspicion. "Please tell me you didn't persuade Samuels to go easy on me." Her arms akimbo, and an eyebrow raised, she waited for his answer.

"Absolutely not." He stared dead in her eye. "The

reason for your early retirement from the Corps is sealed due to the top-secret nature of the mission you were on in Mali." He leaned forward. "But your stellar record is not and that's the data Vince based his hiring decision on."

Kacie tried to hide her relief, but her rigid shoulders sagged. She'd wondered how much the team knew about her past and why she left the Marine Corps after eleven years of service. *Would they trust me if they knew? Would anyone want me to be assigned to their case? I'll work hard to put the past behind me and prove my worth to this group.*

The sergeant stood and put his glass on the counter, then grabbed Kacie's glass and placed it next to his. "Let's get to work, shall we? This place is a mess and violates Marine Corps standards."

He must have noticed her mental drift. His use of humor snapped her out of the painful past. His classic move. "The boxes are marked with the room they go to." She offered him a warm smile and a thumbs-up. "Priority One is locating my hoodies."

****

Monday morning started with a very different drive than Kacie normally experienced. The fast-paced, steady stream of expensive electric cars on California's I-5 transformed into gas-powered pickup trucks with gun racks accelerating around the many curves. *Fine with me.* She pressed on the gas pedal of her white muscle car and leaned into the sharp curve behind a truck with a bed large enough for a tiny house. When Kacie merged onto the straight two-lane highway, she accelerated again. Winding Creek, located outside of Denver, was the ideal suburb for city workers but she opted for a residence with land on the outskirts of the small town. When she joined the Marines, she left her beloved German shepherd, Geronimo, with her parents. Sadly, he died while she was overseas. Another companion like Geronimo would fill an empty space in the solitary journey that had become her life.

Kacie didn't know what to expect on her first day at Bolton's Valor Security and Investigations, but the friendly greetings and fist bumps as she entered the building made her feel right at home. The first person she connected with at the company, a female coworker, Jacy McClain, handed her a cup of coffee and a genuine smile.

"This way." Jacy nodded her head in the direction of the conference room.

They chatted as they walked down the hall covered in framed awards and military citations. She glanced at the names. They belonged to the team members. Jacy apparently noticed her perusal.

"We'll add yours." She hesitated, then added, "I'm certain you have a box full."

"One or two," Kacie said, remembering the Navy Cross being given to her by the Secretary of the Navy while she stood in front of him, forcing a smile. Her hands shook and her knees almost buckled but she managed to stand at attention as he pinned the coveted medal on her blouse.

When she rounded the corner into the conference room, Vince Samuels sat in a high-backed leather chair at the head of the long oak table. He waved her in and pointed to a chair next to him. *If he had an Indian name, it would be, 'Man of Few Words.'* She chuckled to herself at the thought.

Jacy sat beside her and slid a folder down to the boss, then intertwined her fingers and rested her hands on the table. There was no chitchat. Both eyes were focused on Vince. Kacie picked up the nuance of formality that comes from military experience and followed Jacy's lead.

"You have your first assignment." He opened the folder and scanned the first page. "You like dogs?"

"Love them, sir."

"Well, one's gone missing." He tapped the end of his pen on the desk. "We're being tasked with getting her back."

"A missing dog is my first assignment, sir?"

"Kidnapped, actually." He gazed at her for a few seconds, then continued. "The client is a former British SAS soldier I met in Afghanistan. Good dude. He needs our help."

Kacie kept her mien neutral but her thoughts stampeded. *Was this some kind of test? Did he doubt her competence for a real assignment?* She searched his face for a twitch of tease or other tell but his expression remained deadpan.

"Questions?" Vince raised his eyebrows.

"You mentioned he was Special Air Service with experience in Afghanistan."

"True."

"Wouldn't a commando be able to recruit a couple of his Special Forces buddies and retrieve his own dog from a kidnapper?" She waved her hand in the air. "Or hey, how about simply call the police?"

"Without question. But this guy, his name is Trevor Marlowe by the way, is recovering from serious injuries sustained during a hostage rescue. His convalescence will take a while longer."

"Makes sense. Any other data drop you want to offer?" She dropped a hint of cynicism in her tone.

"The dog is his service dog, Freya, who he depends on for sight as his eyes were damaged from an IED blast."

"Is he blind?"

"No, but there is partial loss of visual acuity."

"This keeps getting better and better." Her judgement suggested she tone down the cynicism, but she sensed her new boss was engaged in a game of feeding a starving man pieces of bread. She leaned across the space between them, her eyes steady on his face, and grabbed the folder. Light crinkles around his eyes appeared as his smile grew.

"I knew I made the right decision hiring you, Kacie."

"Thank you, sir." She stood, the folder pressed to her chest and turned to go. "I'll have this memorized cover to cover by tomorrow."

"Burn the rubber home to pack, Marine. You're flying out today at noon."

"The client isn't in Denver?" Surprised, she opened the folder and using her right index finger, flipped through the briefing. "Virginia? He lives in Northern Virginia?" She did a double take at a line in the writeup. "He lives with his father who's a British diplomat? I thought you had agents all over the country?"

"We do but I told him I'd sent my most qualified investigator. You'll need to hit the ground running. The dog was kidnapped late yesterday afternoon." He stood and folded his arms. "Jacy will book your travel and arrange for firepower at the other end. I take it your concealed carry is current?"

"Yes, but the dognapers are probably looking for reward money, not a firefight."

"These guys wore balaclavas and were armed with automatic weapons."

"Now there's a bona fide twist, sir."

"Welcome aboard and screw addressing me as sir. It's Vince."

Chapter Two

Trevor Marlowe was a man who excelled at running toward danger. He slammed his metal cane into the wood paneling of the den. He didn't like having to sit on the sidelines, especially when his gut told him the threat was personal. These men were not ordinary dognapers. After the call came in from his groomer that two heavily armed men in balaclavas forced their way into her studio and stole his service dog right off the grooming table, he loaded his sniper rifle and raced for the door. But when a little voice called out from the stairwell and asked him if was going to kill someone, he froze. His six-year-old daughter's question impinged on him and forced the memory of his wife, who died of cancer two years prior. He was the sole parent responsible for her safety and she needed him alive.

"Emma, darling, Dad is going to look for Freya." He checked that the safety was on and lowered the rifle, leaning it in the corner.

"Hazel will stay with you until I get back." He knelt and held out his arms.

She ran to his embrace. "Did she run away, Dad?"

He didn't want to alarm her, but he promised his wife he'd always be honest with her and their daughter. Or as honest as his top-secret clearance would allow. As a former British Special Air Service member, many of his absences had the added impact of secrecy. His wife had helped soften the blow of how long Dad would be gone and executed brilliant distraction methods like baking cookies or trips to the zoo. *What's my strategy? Freya didn't run away. A couple of dirt bags stole her.*

"Freya left the groomer early and got lost, but we'll find her."

"Can I help?"

"Yes." He pointed to the bay window in the living room. "Color in your book and watch for her."

Emma released her grip on his shoulders. "Freya is so smart. She'll come home." She picked up her coloring book and crayons. "Let's bake cookies for her like Mum and I did when we wanted you to come home." Her hands connected with an excited clap.

His chest tightened. He pushed himself off the floor and twisted in a half turn so she wouldn't see the tears poised to overflow down his cheeks. He loved serving his country and thrived as a member of the British Special Forces for many years, but his last mission resulted in his left tricep muscle being shot halfway off, a crippling knife wound in his leg and partial loss of vision. It was a wake-up call. No way would he turn precious Emma into an orphan. He swiped his cheek, then faced Emma with a forced smile.

"I think Freya would like a steak. I'll ask Hazel to add it to the grocery list."

"Is Hazel our family?"

"She's our housekeeper but we like her like family."

"Hazel is nice to me." She twirled a strand of her hair.

Trevor cupped her chin. "I love you, my sweet girl."

He checked his watch. His friend at the private investigation service would still be at work. "Emma, do Dad a favor. Find Hazel and ask her if she can stay on duty late tonight and help with dinner. I need to make a phone call."

Trevor waited until his daughter scampered out of earshot then punched in the cell number for one of the few American military partners he'd stayed in contact with since his deployment to Afghanistan. He and Vince Samuels shared a joint operation where his position as overwatch saved the dude's life. The Green Beret had later texted him an image of a business card listing out the name and address of an investigative service. Included was a note that said, "If you ever need a favor, brother."

"Yo, brother. What's up?"

"I'm calling to collect on that favor."

"Does it have anything to do with your last deployment to Africa? I heard you got into some shit."

"News does make its way through the notorious, secret halls of the Special Forces community."

"I see you haven't lost your dry British humor." He snorted a laugh.

"No, you snake eater. Just half my tricep and ability to chase the bloody arseholes that stole my service dog." His tone punched hard.

"Dognapers? Couldn't the local uniforms handle that?"

"Yes, unless it's armed blokes in combat attire, hiding their identity with balaclavas." He hesitated. "I can send you more detail in an encrypted email."

"Do that stat. We'll jump on this like stink on poopy."

"How fast can you get the investigator here?"

"Tomorrow evening. I'll send my best."

"Thanks, man."

"Stay frosty."

The conversation ended but Trevor's confidence for resolution rebounded from the dark drag of despair he'd experienced after the groomer's panicked phone call from a few hours earlier. When you serve with a guy in combat or even tough training, you soon learn the constitution of that soldier. He experienced Vince firsthand as a guy you could count on to have your back. Trevor was confident the most experienced badass tracker would soon be hot on the trail of who stole Freya.

****

Without Freya's soft snore to lull him to sleep, Trevor spent the night wrapped and unwrapped in the cotton sheets of his queen bed. Sometime after midnight, Emma wandered into his bedroom and crawled into the empty space left by the eighty-pound German shepherd.

A friend had given her a stuffed replica of Freya, which she slept with every night. The dog served the family above and beyond. Although she was assigned to him as a service dog, she'd become an integral member of the family. The fact that the kidnappers tranked her, pissed him off. According to the groomer, she didn't go willingly and put up a worthy fight. *I'll find you, Freya. Whatever it takes.*

The first beams of sunlight peeked through the blinds, signaling the dawn of a new day. Trevor rolled over to gaze at Emma, curled in a ball around her stuffed toy. He stroked her fine red hair and mouthed, 'I love you,' before easing his way out of bed. With a second glance at the doorway, he headed downstairs for a hot black tea and preparation.

His father's housekeeper, Hazel, stood shaking at the bottom of the stairs, paler than her usual Welsh complexion. With her left hand braced on the banister, she held a folded piece of paper in her other outstretched hand. Hazel had been his nanny as a young man and, out of loyalty to his family, accompanied his father to America when he was assigned to the Diplomatic Corp. She was never at a loss for words.

"What's wrong?" Trevor steadied her hand as he retrieved the note. She pointed to the front door, her eyes wide. He noticed the top lock was disengaged as if someone had opened the door. There was a brown manila envelope on the floor with the top torn open.

"Speak, woman," he commanded. "What's going on?"

"A teenaged boyyy drop...ped thissss off and asked meeee to give it to you." She stuttered the words, then swallowed hard before continuing. "He s-said a guy who spoke w-with an accent paid him twenty d-dollars to deliver it."

Trevor unfolded the note and squinted at the writing. As he read the message, his temple pounded from the heightened pulse.

"Bloody hell." He glared at Hazel as he shook the paper. "A ransom note!" He swung open the door and stepped onto the front porch. His gaze darted from left to right.

"I wouldn't pry into your mail but he said it was

urgent." Hazel stepped over the threshold and started to cry.

"I'm not mad at you." Trevor turned and wrapped his arm around her shoulder. "But I'm pissed at the savagery of them finding where I live and coming to my father's house."

"What are you going to do?" Hazel wrung her hands. "Their ransom demand of five hundred thousand dollars within twenty-four hours sounds impossible."

"I'm not certain if I pay the money, I'll get Freya back alive." He shook his head.

"There's also the kidnapper's condition of no police and no press." She sniffed back tears.

"They don't want me to have a safety net but I have plans already in motion." He released his grip and moved to relock the door.

"What can I do to help?"

"Don't let Emma out of your sight and don't open the door to anyone unless you know them." He stooped to peer deep into her eyes. "Be cool. I don't want Emma any more worried than she already is."

She nodded. "Do you want me to notify your father?"

"Not necessary at this point. He's in Canada, with a security detail."

Hazel straightened her shoulders and jutted her chin out. "I'm going to fix some tea for you. I'll bring it to your office."

"Thanks." He patted her on the shoulder and smiled. "One more thing. I'm expecting a visitor. Young and female. She'll arrive sometime this morning."

"Oh, Trevor. This is quite unexpected." She tittered

The Heart of Valor

as she wiped her hands on her apron.

"It's not what you think. I hired an investigator to help find Freya. The agency claimed they're sending the person with the most experience for this assignment. That's all."

"Well, I hope she's easy on the eyes." She winked at Trevor.

"I couldn't tell much from the photo attached to her profile. She was in uniform, and her hat covered most of her face. I couldn't even tell if she had hair, it was so stuffed up under her hat."

"Whatever you say, my boy." She turned and headed into the kitchen; a quiet whistle emanated from her lips.

"Glad you're feeling better," he quipped, then crinkled the note in a ball and entered his office.

Trevor understood the most successful military operations depended on laying the groundwork for an assault. Seated at his desk, he texted a familiar number.
—*Have a job. Need is immediate. Check for encrypted email.* —

Although the agent Vince was sending looked great on paper with ten plus years of investigative experience, he'd never worked with her before and wasn't taking any chances. The two chaps he hired would shadow her and run interference, which was a nice way of saying use lethal force if necessary.

Out of his peripheral vision he noticed Hazel crossing the threshold into his office with a tray. He assumed it held a hot cup of tea and a couple of hard-boiled eggs. Just as she rested the platter on the desk, the doorbell rang. Hazel leapt cat-like off the ground.

"Good thing you already put the bloody tray

down." He chuckled as he stood. "You stay here. I'll check the door."

Trevor drew back the curtain in the office. A female figure waited on the front stoop. He couldn't make out the face as her back was turned but her shape was noticeably athletic with a cute bubble butt tightly packed in the Marpat cargo pants. With a thumbs-up to Hazel indicating the visitor was friend not foe, he walked to the door. A glance in the mirror next to the entrance reminded him he hadn't done his morning ablutions. He hardly recognized the unruly haired, stubble face staring back. *I don't need to impress her. I need to find my dog.* Trevor swung open the door with a whoosh and jolted from surprise. An exceedingly attractive woman stood before him with her hand outstretched for a shake.

"Mr. Marlowe? Hi, I'm Kacie O'Shea from Valor Security." She removed her baseball cap with her free hand and long blonde tresses, which had been neatly tucked under the hat, fell in waves down her back.

"Charmed, I'm sure." He shoved his right hand into hers and experienced a firm grip with direct eye contact from eyes the color of rich coffee. "Please, come in." He stepped aside and waved his arm in welcome. As she entered, close enough for him to capture the alluring scent of lavender, the word 'hottie' thumped around in his head. He likened her to an Instagram model, not a combat savvy warrior. "Would you like something to drink or eat?"

"No, I'm good and ready to get to work finding your dog, sir." She brushed aside her bangs.

"We can step into my office." He held out his hand, indicating a room to the left of the entrance. "I'll brief you and by the way, feel free to call me Trevor." She nodded as she passed in front of him. He conveyed a *what the hell* expression to Hazel, who had joined them.

"This is Hazel. She takes care of us."

"Nice to meet you, Hazel." Kacie smiled. "You keep a lovely home."

"Thank you, dear." She fussed with her apron and tittered. "I must admit you don't fit the tough, weathered image I had of a U.S. Marine."

"We come in all sizes and both sexes but I assure you the standards don't vary. We all come out Semper Fi." She winked with an exaggerated tilt of her head.

"Mr. Marlowe. Uh, Trevor, you mentioned us. Who else lives here?" She retrieved a pad of paper and pen from her back pocket and stood poised to take notes.

"My daughter and I are temporarily staying here with my father, who is out of the country, so Hazel can help me recover and also help with Emma."

A small voice floated in from the hall. "Is she going to help us find Freya, Dad?"

"Yes, darling. Come in and say hello."

Emma skipped into the room and went straight up to Kacie. "You're pretty."

"Why, thank you, Emma. So are you."

Trevor rubbed the stubble on his chin, suddenly self-conscious about the fact he hadn't showered or shaved.

"Hazel, will you help Emma cook breakfast and get ready for school?"

"Certainly." She herded the girl out of the room.

Trevor shut the door. "I'll give you the current sitrep."

Chapter Three

Kacie arrived at Dapper Dog Grooming in McLean, Virginia, a few minutes earlier than her GPS indicated. She viewed this as a good omen. The location was in an upscale shopping center with gray-painted brick facades and red and white striped awnings. She scanned to the right and left of the shop, centered between a fancy boutique and specialty coffee store.

How did two men in camo and, from the sound of it, automatic weapons, wearing balaclavas not get noticed? There's a chill in the air at night but during the day, overcoats, even light jackets, would look conspicuous.

She sat for a few minutes observing the clientele. Most of them were buried in their cell phones, talking or texting.

Bingo! A purple elephant could march through the parking lot and half these people wouldn't notice.

She drove around to the alley behind the store where the dirtbags had exited with the dog and parked her rental car. There were two exits out of the alley, one north and one south.

Kacie glanced at her notes. The owner, Annabelle Sinclair, didn't try to rescue the dog or follow the creeps outside. Smart lady. According to Trevor, she resided in the same neighborhood as his family. As a favor, she picked up and returned Freya. Trevor adamantly ruled out any possibility of Annabelle's involvement. She'd accept his endorsement for now. It was possible they had been surveilling the groomer and followed the driver to the Marlowe house. The added convenience of drop off could have been how the thugs discovered where Trevor lived.

But how did they know the dog belonged to Trevor? Or that Annabelle groomed Freya? A potential string to pull.

Kacie scanned the outside of the building and breathed a sigh of relief. Cameras were installed in several key positions, with one trained on the back door and one which might identify the type of vehicle they were driving. With her trained eyes, she inspected the area outside the back door as well as the alley way for any evidence of the crime. There was a bloody handprint on the door. It appeared fresh enough for DNA analysis.

Freya didn't go quietly. Good girl.

She ducked back into her car and retrieved her portable fingerprint kit. After capturing the prints, she neatly tucked them away until she could get it sent overnight to headquarters to run through their system. Rather than spook the owner by banging on the back door, she decided to drive around to the front. She had one foot in her car when she spotted something shiny parallel to the bottom stair and swung back out. Kacie smiled as she bent to confirm what she thought was a syringe.

My good fortune. It must have fallen out of the vehicle or bag as they wrestled with Freya.

She pulled nitrile gloves out of her back pocket and

carefully lifted the syringe by the handle. Holding it up to the light, she could see a few drops of liquid still inside. She placed the hypodermic needle inside a sterile plastic bag and then inside the fingerprint kit for safekeeping.

The back door swung open with a bang. Surprised by the sudden movement, she reached for her concealed weapon until a stunning twenty something female rounded the corner and waved.

"You must be the person Trevor hired. I observed you in the security cameras," she said, pointing to the camera above the door. "I'm Annabelle."

Kacie released her weapon. "Hi. I'm Kacie."

"I assumed you were the person Trevor called me about." With a warm smile, she flipped her thick black curls off her shoulder.

"Come in. I'm sure you want to review the security cameras." She waved her hand, inviting Kacie inside.

The investigator in Kacie suggested Annabelle might be more than a casual family friend and might be grooming more than the dog, but it explained Trevor's adamant denial the beautiful Annabelle had any involvement in the kidnapping. Noted.

****

After returning to her hotel room at the posh Banbridge Suites in McLean, Kacie reviewed the security footage from Dapper Dog Groomers. *Voila.* A clear image of the make and model and a blurred but readable tag number of the van as it sped from the scene. She grabbed her phone and willed her hand to stop shaking as she scrolled through contacts for the data analysis-intel guy at headquarters. Gilbert O'Shaughnessy was a brilliant analyst who served as an

Army Intelligence officer specializing in covert operations. A whip smart guy with a wicked sense of humor who apparently had a penchant for athletic blondes. "I know a little café if you ever want to get hammered together," was his intro on her first day of employment.

"Speak," he said.

"Hi, Gil. It's Kacie. I need your help."

"Did you submit a DA form 3161?" His tone was serious and formal.

"No one told me I had to submit a form." Frustrated by the idea of a delay, she continued. "I'm on assignment. It's urgent." She matched his all-business tone.

"Gotcha, sweetheart. I'm at your service." He chuckled.

"You sound delighted at tripping me up, you asshole." She mocked his chuckle.

"Now I'm getting aroused." His voice rumbled.

"I'm going to start calling you 'Cheesy Gil' for obvious reasons."

"Well, at least you'll call me," he said with a flirty air.

"If you help me solve this case, I'll do much more than call you," she purred.

"I'm all ears, beautiful, and I promise to keep my hands to myself."

"Uncross your fingers, Gil." She laughed, then proceeded to brief him on the evidence she'd gathered so far.

"Great work," he said with the interest of someone who delighted in his work of solving data puzzles.

"I'm headed to FedEx after we hang up so be on

the lookout for the package. I'll send it to arrive before ten a.m."

"Will do, and you be on the lookout for an unusually large package when you get home."

"OMG! Gil. Goodbye for now. Call with the license data ASAP." She shook her head and thought of a new nickname. 'Gutter Gil.' She smiled as she grabbed her purse and a dark hoodie.

Kacie expected Gil to text her the address for the tag quickly and when he did, she'd head straight to the target area. Other than the fact the nappers tranked the dog, she didn't have any idea what condition Freya would be in when found. She had packed a cooler with water, food and antibiotics. If she had to throw a stitch, she also carried a medical kit.

After the overnight drop off, Kacie texted her boss to check in. Then, she called Trevor to apprise him of forward motion on the investigation. He seemed pleased but acted cagey when she brought up the ransom note and whether he'd heard from the kidnappers. It reminded her of a past boyfriend who would lie to her but said he hated doing it. Something was up. While Trevor had sought her advice about how to handle the ransom note, she had a gut reaction he disagreed with not paying it. Her stomach did somersaults during the conversation. She understood the guy desperately wanted his dog back but she counted on his cooperation. Otherwise, her life and Freya's could be put in danger.

Her phone dinged and an address appeared along with a stern warning from Gil. "Location west of you in Culpepper, Virginia. Careful approach. Owner of van traced to bad, bad dude with ties to the extremist group,

Boko Haram. Head on a swivel. Seek and destroy, Jarhead."

Kacie plugged the address into her GPS and viewed the map.

Way out of town and dusk is approaching.

According to her GPS, the drive would take her an hour and a half. With one hand on the wheel and one left to rummage in her purse, she retrieved the high-intensity flashlight she considered a necessity and placed it on the passenger seat. This assignment just transformed from a simple kidnapping to a high-risk mission.

Once outside of the ambient light of the city limits and after she turned off I-66, the roads became high-beam dark. Unfamiliar with the area but driven by her desire to rescue Trevor's canine, despite the recent elevation of danger, she shoved the pedal to the metal. Her mind skipped through details of a tentative plan once she arrived at the location. Other than the fact it appeared to be out in the country, she didn't have a clue what she was facing. She did have, however, a who. 'Unfriendlies' with terrorist ties could be waiting. The landscape whipped by as she glanced at the map on her dashboard. *I'm getting close.*

The voice navigation announced a right-hand turn off the main road in point two miles. Kacie slowed the car and strained to see ahead, but a tall, dense hedge lined the side of the road.

The GPS directed her to turn onto the street listed as the address for the owner of the van. Unpaved, the road inclined up toward a desolate property nestled in a stand of large oaks. A light pole offered a silhouette view of a small wood-framed house with a wide front porch perched alone at the top of the hill.

Wary and alert, she crept along the street past the driveway, until a sign that said, 'Dead End, No Exit''' appeared. The road was too narrow and the shoulder too steep to initiate a U-turn, so she backed up into a neighbor's gravel driveway and turned around. As she approached the target house, she doused her headlights and rolled into the entrance. She backed behind the hedges, for a fast and easy exit, and cut off the engine.

The place appeared deserted, but she'd been down this road before during her last tour of duty. It had all the signs of an ambush. With a deep breath, she grabbed her flashlight and exited. The 9mm, usually tucked in her purse, now hung from her hip in a Kydex holster, her hand on the grip as she used the hedge for cover and crouched low toward the main structure. After she ascended the hill, a small red barn, located behind the house, came into view. A light shone through the rectangular window at the top of the structure. Curious, she changed course and made her way to the back of the barn. She checked her surroundings for possible company. No movement. Too quiet. There was a major padlock on a double chain securing the doors.

Too bad I left my hacksaw at home.

She pulled a compact metal box from her cargo pants. *Lucky for me, I opted in for the lock picking course.*

With her flashlight secured between her teeth, she proceeded to pop the heavy lock. As soon as she wrestled the unwieldy chain out of the iron handles, a soft whimpering commenced. She turned off the flashlight and stuffed it in her pocket.

The oak doors were heavy and would be loud when opened, but she opted for speed and with both arms, she slid one of the doors to the side as fast as she could muster. A beautiful but groggy sable colored German Shepherd Dog peered at her through guarded eyes. The dog seemed unsteady, most likely still under the effects of tranquilizers. She appeared to be about eighty pounds and might be too heavy to carry. Kacie started toward the dog in a slow careful gait and called out her name.

"Freya, I'm here to help." The dog lifted her head in recognition of her name. Kacie extended her hand so Freya could acquire her scent, although she didn't know if smell alone would be enough to gain her trust. Luckily, she brought one of Trevor's unwashed socks with her which she retrieved from her pants pocket and dangled in front of the canine. Freya's attention focused on the sock and her tail wagged. Kacie knelt and touched the dog's head while visually checking her for any obvious injury but found none. Nearby, bowls of food and water sat untouched.

Confident the shepherd would not attack with her nose deep in Trevor's sock, Kacie reached under her carriage and tried to lift her to a standing position. She wobbled but her attention stayed riveted on the sock. Freya steadied herself. Kacie secured the leash on Freya's collar and tied the smelly sock to her waistband. The window for her exfil was closing. She needed to move before the tangos returned but the possibility of Freya being dehydrated weighed on her. She cupped water in her palm and patted Freya's mouth with the liquid. Freya lapped a few mouthfuls of water, wagged her tail as if in acknowledgement. The dog seemed steadier.

"Ready, girl? Let's get the hell out of here." She led Freya out the back, rounded the corner of the barn, and stepped into the darkness, allowing her eyes to adjust.

A low growl from Freya snapped her attention in the direction of the driveway and her escape route. Two men in military-styled clothing, armed with rifles, approached the front of the barn, moving in a combat crouch. She drew her weapon. As the men crept into the spreading light from the barn's upper window, she froze. They wore camouflage pants with black t-shirts, same as shown in the security tapes from the groomer and, although not masked, she couldn't get a clear view of what they looked like with baseball caps pulled low over their faces.

Outnumbered and outgunned, with the clear conclusion they'd seen her car, she decided surprise was her only option, but when she stepped forward, a flashback from her past deployment bombarded her thoughts. She couldn't think, couldn't move. Her throat tightened. Suddenly parched and unable to swallow, her body frozen in panic, she gathered every ounce of mental strength to reclaim her composure and regain her battle balance.

A wet nose nudged her hand. She glanced at Freya, who gazed at her with questioning eyes. *I can't let her or my team down by failing.*

She compartmentalized and focused. The memories, like demons, were banished from her mind. With her gun drawn, she assumed a firing position and shot each man with one round.

Chapter Four

"C'mon, Freya, you can make it," Kacie said, as she tugged gently at the dog's leash while glancing over her shoulder at the messy scene behind her. She'd managed to wound both guys. The way they fell told her where the bullets hit. The taller man took one in his right leg and crumpled to the ground, screaming in agony, while the second, heavier guy fell backward, arms flailing outward from impact to his chest.

Freya, frightened by the sound of gunfire, trembled so violently she could barely move. Cognizant of the brief window she had to exit, Kacie holstered her weapon and shoveled the German Shepherd up in her arms. Freya's heartbeat raced and her tongue lolled out as Kacie jogged down the driveway. Voices yelling out curse words followed her descent. She hesitated for a second before placing Freya in the backseat. One of the accents sounded oddly British. Still hyper-focused on the threat, she brushed her thoughts aside and drove her rented SUV like a Formula 1 car until she reached civilization. After she checked the rearview and observed only streetlights lining empty lanes, she slowed her speed. With one hand on the wheel, she reached back to pet Freya, who licked her palm. A well-lit gas station next to a busy fast-food restaurant offered good cover and a view of the road in both directions. She pulled into the parking lot and parked. Freya sat up, ears forward.

"Good girl." Kacie sighed a slow breath, but still planned to suggest Trevor take her to a veterinarian. The tranquilizers she'd been given were no joke. Kacie filled a small bowl from her kit with water and offered it to Freya. She heard lapping as she dialed the number for her boss.

"Mission complete, sir," Kacie said with a smile. She held the phone over the back seat so Vince could hear Freya lap up the water.

"Yes. I can hear your compliance." He laughed. "Good job, Kacie. Now, report."

Kacie briefed him with all the details of the rescue, including the hostile confrontation at the barn. She offered to call Trevor but Vince said he'd relay the good news, and suggested she head straight for his home. She checked her watch. It was close to ten p.m.

"It'll be close to eleven before I get there."

"He wants his dog back. I'll let him know your ETA."

She started the engine. "On my way."

****

Trevor swung open the door and smiled as Kacie dropped her finger aimed at the doorbell.

"You must have been looking out the window," Kacie said before Trevor could speak. "She's okay."

"Where is she?" Trevor peered over Kacie's head at the rental in his driveway.

"Asleep in the back." She nodded her head toward the SUV. "Freya's a wonderful dog. I can understand why she means so much to you."

"Not just me." His throat tightened. "Emma has grown very attached to her since her mother passed away." For a moment his mind shifted to the days after his wife died. He'd been consumed by the emptiness, and the grief. Then the anger and regret settled in. His solution had been to throw himself into the pit of hell and volunteer for a tier one covert mission in Africa. He told Emma not to worry. Daddy was going to work but he'd be back and bring her a surprise. By the grace of God, he made it home. Thanks to a friend with connections to the Dogs for Warriors Foundation, an eight-week-old Freya was Emma's surprise. The canine had been placed with him as a service dog, but Emma claimed the German Shepherd as her own. He swore the dog comprehended the truth but she played her role believably and with complete devotion to his little girl.

A light grip on his arm brought him back to the present. He stared into the soft brown eyes peering up at him, scanning his expression with a gentle understanding. He reached for Kacie and drew her into a hug. She returned the embrace. Her warmth swept over him as the scent of lavender pervaded his senses. He wanted to kiss her. Reaching down, he lifted her chin and noticed her lips part in a welcome. With his heart racing, he leaned in and barely touched her lips when the door banged opened.

"Oh, I didn't mean to interrupt," Annabelle said with a tinge of sarcasm.

Kacie stepped back and slipped off the top stair but Trevor caught her before she fell further. "I've got you." He tugged her back on the first step and held on to her arm.

"Thanks." She gave him a brief smile, then pulled her arm out of his grasp.

"I brought Freya home," Kacie said to Annabelle.

"Oh, thank God." She gazed up at Trevor briefly, then addressed Kacie. "That was fast."

"Your security cameras gave me the breakthrough necessary and I got lucky." She glanced at Trevor. "My boss will be sending you a complete debrief on the rescue within the next twenty-four hours. Let's go get Freya."

Damn. The 'all business face' returns but still so beautiful. "Yes. Let's. I'm certain she's hungry and tired and ready for her doggo bed."

"I can stay if you need me," Annabelle said, with a coy tilt of her head.

"Thanks, Annabelle. I believe the best medicine for her right now is rest and quiet and me."

"I would agree with that prescription." Kacie fiddled with the strings on her hoodie, then added, "I also recommend you take her to a veterinarian tomorrow." She held up her index finger. "Just as a precaution."

Trevor hobbled down the handicapped ramp as fast as he could, holding the black metal rail to steady himself and propel himself forward. Kacie turned and raced down the steps and beat him to the rental. She opened the back door when he approached. His stomach dropped. Freya sat up, filling the space, her tail wagging in big sweeps. He braced himself against the door jam and hugged her. Tears he tried to hold back, fell freely down his cheeks. He'd been taught that crying in public was a sign of weakness. With his face buried in Freya's neck, he choked out a greeting.

"Good girl. Who's my good girl?" He scratched her ears while he collected his emotions. Using his hands, he swiped along her body and down her legs for any obvious injury. "I'll bet you're knackered."

Kacie gathered the items she'd brought to care for the dog after her rescue, walked them up to the front porch, and handed them to Annabelle.

He guessed she was giving him space rather than walking away from a lack of empathy. A sudden urge struck him. He hadn't talked to anyone about his injury, hadn't felt the need–until now. With a light tug on the leash, Freya leapt from the car and shoved her head between Trevor's legs. He lost his balance and fell backward on the concrete with a hard thud.

"You, okay?" Kacie's face peered over him.

"Yeah, damn bum leg gave out when Freya bumped me."

Kacie clasped his hand and pulled him upright. His chest smacked into her full bosom. The heat from his arousal spread from the pit of his stomach to his groin. He didn't retreat. He let desire dictate his actions and wrapped his arms around her back. Her gaze flicked to the front door and she stiffened in his arms. He backed away. *Damn. Twice in one day.*

"As you can see, Kacie, Trevor's a very generous man," Annabelle's voice dripped with hostility. "At least I've found him to be so."

The message could not have been clearer although he had failed to read it earlier. Annabelle's jealousy annoyed him and intentionally sent the wrong message to Kacie. He'd had no relations with her or any woman since his wife died. Kacie's miffed expression said she believed him to be a cad.

"Take good care of them both, Annabelle," she said as she hopped into her SUV. With a brief wave, she backed out of the driveway and sped down the street.

"Go home, Annabelle." Pissed, Trevor grabbed Freya's lead and limped back into the house. For the first time in as long as he could remember, he wanted someone. He wanted Kacie.

****

The long flight home gave Kacie space to reflect on her assignment and the close call with Trevor. Her contract with the agency clearly stated that becoming romantically involved with a client was a no-no. Well, not in those exact words but listed it as a reason for termination.

She'd seen a picture of him in the file the agency provided and took note of his obvious good looks, but when he answered the door, she swallowed a gasp. His sandy brown hair fell in an unruly curl over his forehead, directing her attention to the most intense cobalt blue eyes she'd ever seen. The facial scruff hid his expression, but his eyes smiled as he surveyed her face. The connection, like an electric shock, jumpstarted her emotions and cracked the flawless public façade she'd maintained to conceal a less pleasant reality after her last tour of duty.

As soon as the tires of the plane bumped on the landing strip, she started her phone and punched in the number to her First Sergeant and texted —*Just landed. Defcon 2. When can we talk?* — With her eyes glued to the screen, and a gorilla grip on the phone case, she waited. The minutes dragged by like those last thirty minutes of school before summer vacation. Finally, a notification of a message.

—*Defcon 2? What shit show have you gotten yourself involved in?* —

A smile spread across her lips. As usual, First Sergeant Crockett understood without knowing any details. She replied, —*Love is in the air like a broccoli fart.* — She wasn't trying to communicate in code but if she was honest, it fit.

—*Oh, thank God. I thought you killed someone.* —

A chuckle bubbled up from her chest. —*Maimed, not killed but that was intentional. The other not so much.* —

— *For fuck's sake, get to somewhere private and call me.* —

— *Hungry? I'll treat at our favorite burger joint.* — She added a smiley face emoji.

—*On my way. Your ETA?* —

— *Be there in thirty.* —

She placed the phone back in the suction cup stand as a thumbs-up emoji appeared from Crockett.

When Kacie pulled into the parking lot, Crockett's dark blue pickup was in the front spot next to the door. This late in the afternoon, the lunch crowd had eaten and the early bird seniors weren't due for another hour. They'd have plenty of privacy. She parked next to him and checked herself in the mirror. He was meticulous about grooming, and although there had never been any romantic vibes between them, she considered him her mentor. Driven by respect, she smoothed down her hair and tucked a few loose strands behind her ears before exiting her Mustang. As she entered the restaurant, she scanned the room. He'd be in the farthest booth with his back against the wall, hands folded and elbows resting on the table. *Bingo.* He beckoned her with a smile that was all perfect white teeth. When she approached, he slid out of the booth with the graceful confidence of a lion and embraced her with a hearty hug.

She dropped her head on his chest, wrapped her arms around his waist, and squeezed. The steady rhythm of his heartbeat soothed her nerves. While in the Marine Corps, he'd served as her mentor and guided her through the minefield of being an active-duty Marine. His highway of experience had many more miles than hers and she trusted his advice. Nothing changed after she left the Corps. They had an honest to God connection she hoped would last a lifetime.

He disengaged from her hold and held her at arm's length while he inspected her face. A frown embedded in his dark-skinned forehead deepened. She understood his concern over her effusiveness. No one described her as a hugger or one who emoted freely. Her acts of affection were usually a slap on the arm or a sideways hug, but only after the invitation to, 'bring it in' and a few beers.

"The mission was successful," she said flatly. "I retrieved the kidnapped dog and shot the two dudes who took her."

"Well done, I think," he said with a puzzled expression. "Did you get into a firefight?"

"Unfortunately." She swept her bangs back. "These guys weren't normal kidnappers. They had military grade gear and from the little bit I heard one of them spoke with a British accent."

He gazed into the distance briefly, then signaled they should sit. "That's odd. Have you had your debrief with the boss yet?"

"No. I called Vince to report the mission success but didn't give him details. I'll do that in person. I can't say he didn't warn me about the threat level, though."

She tilted her head. "Why? What's ruminating in that big brain of yours?"

"I think there's more to the dognapping than you were told." He leaned forward, placing his elbows on the table.

"You mean than Vince told me or Trevor told Vince?"

"I think Trevor's holding out." He paused as the waitress appeared at the table and asked if they were ready to order.

"You know what you want?" he asked.

"My usual, Akashi beef cheeseburger," she said peering up at the familiar waitress with a smile. "With unsweetened tea."

"Same." He nodded to the waitress, waiting until she was out of earshot to continue. "Freya has value to Trevor as a service dog but she's not a priceless piece of art. Normal kidnappers are money motivated. How much wealth do you suppose a career military guy would acquire?"

"Are you saying this is more about his diplomat father?"

"Maybe, but if he was a target, one of the governments would have obtained Intel about it and strengthened his protection wall as well as the family's."

"I agree. Then, what?"

"Trevor is a public figure and well known in his capture and kill of a prominent Boko Haram terrorist leader in Africa. He also rescued hostages from a hotel in Kenya held by members of the different but equally dangerous group. He's a celebrity in the Special Forces community and a declared enemy to Boko Haram leadership."

"You think this was a revenge plot to hurt him by stealing his dog?"

"If that was their intention, you would have found Freya dead."

"They were coming back to the barn when I encountered them. Maybe I foiled their plans to off the dog."

"Possible. My initial hunch was they were checking on the dog and fully planned to make this look like a dognapping so as not to alert anyone to a more sinister plot."

"And now?"

"The British accent throws a wrench into my theory. Boko members would be speaking Arabic or French." He raised an eyebrow. "Any chance this was an inside job?"

"You mean Trevor hired his own men to kidnap the dog?" She vigorously shook her head. "No way he'd put Freya through that kind of ordeal."

"Okay. Then back to theory number one."

"Which is?"

"Kidnap and kill Trevor."

"Revenge." She bobbed her head. "That makes more sense. His injuries make him vulnerable."

"He needs to up his own personal security, in my opinion. You could suggest that as part of your debrief. May give you another opportunity for work." He smiled.

"Uh, that brings us to the real reason I called you." The hot rush of embarrassment rose up her neck and face. "I can't go back."

Crockett's eyebrows shot up. "Do tell."

"Trevor is very charismatic widower. There was an undeniable attraction and he has an adorable daughter." Her words tumbled out in a rush.

"Did he move on you?"

"He almost kissed me."

"What the hell, Kacie." He laughed. "I don't see you as an almost kind of girl."

"I'm not. Believe me, I was going in for the full contact, tongue tango when we got interrupted by his groomer, who has the definite hots for him."

"You've never backed down from a little competition."

"It's not that. My contract with the agency forbids fraternizing with clients. It's grounds for immediate dismissal."

"How did you leave it with Trevor?"

"Tearing-ass down the street in full retreat."

Chapter Five

Trevor, seated in his favorite oversized armchair, stroked Freya's outstretched head, grateful for her return. She snuggled closer to his leg and peered at him with a steady gaze. He noticed a clinginess that hadn't been present before but he understood the reaction.

"You're home now, girl." He forced down the anger dominating his emotions every time he pictured her fear and confusion at being taken. Freya's eyes closed as Trevor placed a few more strategic rubs under the chin. Relaxed enough to doze off, her head bobbed and she leaned into the base of the chair for support.

The door to his study opened and Emma, smiling broadly at the sight of the sable German Shepherd, rushed over, a favored treat in her hand. Startled by the sudden movement, Freya jumped awake with a sharp bark. Emma froze but her gaze darted from the dog to her father. Still holding the treat, she started to cry and dropped the pork chew. Trevor grabbed the handle of Freya's halter, and ordered, "Plotz." The canine dropped to the floor, panting.

"Honey, she's still coping with being kidnapped." He waved her over but Emma refused to move, shaking her head. "Where is my blasted cane?"

Emma wiped her tears and sniffled, then pointed to the large oak staff, which had rolled under the chair on the far side of Freya.

"I need your help, sweetheart. Would you get me my cane?" He kept his voice low and encouraging.

Emma, to her credit, stepped forward and picked up the treat and with an open palm offered it to Freya. The dog stayed in a prone position but gazed at him and wagged her tail. He released her halter.

"Good plotz, girl. Okay," he said with an approving tone, giving her a signal she could release from that position. She stood, ears back and tail wagging. "Emma, darling, let her come to you."

His daughter showed impressive resilience considering everything she'd experienced in her young life. He had a hunch this wasn't about fear but more about hurt that "her dog" had reacted in an unfriendly way.

Emma squatted and called to Freya, who wagged her way to the little girl and took the treat gently out of her hand. Side by side they crawled on all fours and retrieved the cane. As she handed it to her father, she asked, "Can Freya come to my room and play?"

"Of course." He smiled at the return of the familiar routine. "I have to make a phone call so both of you, skedaddle."

Trevor wanted to hear what Kacie had written in her report. Had she included his simmering glances, their brief but intense physical encounter? He doubted it but the image of her filled a sad, empty space in his head. The warmth of her breasts pressed into his chest had him breathing hard. Good God. A trip to Colorado sounded like a recipe for healing. He'd request an in-person briefing with Vince.

****

The clinch in Vince's jaw was an expected

response, validating Trevor's decision to fly to Colorado for an in-person meeting. Trevor had weighed the consequences of telling Vince about the two former army friends he'd employed to act as backup to Kacie and opted for the truth. He assured Vince neither of the men who Kacie wounded had suffered serious injuries, nor would either pursue charges. The Green Beret's demeanor remained intensely disapproving. His friend wasn't buying the justification that Kacie was new to the job and he couldn't take any chances that Freya wouldn't come home. As it turned out, Kacie was better at the job than the two men he hired. She was first on the scene and handled herself like a real pro.

"What the fuck were you thinking, Marlowe?" Vince pounded his fist on the desk. "You could have gotten my operative killed."

"I understand, Vince, but I instructed those gentlemen not to engage if they encountered Kacie and nothing in my contract with your organization prohibited me from increasing my odds at finding my dog."

"She could have killed them," Vince shouted.

"But she didn't," Trevor countered. "Kacie's either a terrible shot or only wanted to slow them down."

"She's an excellent shot, Bucko." Vince rested his forehead into the palm of his hand. "She stated in her report her main objective was to save the dog but added if they had pursued her, all bets were off." He grabbed a page from the printer and after a quick glance at the contents, continued. "It appears there's more to this kidnapping than a simple abduction." Vince picked up a paper and waved it in the air. "Have you received threats to your life?"

"Not directly but through back channels from British intelligence."

"Are they related to your service in Africa?"

"That's the consensus." Trevor nodded. Curious as to the contents on the typed sheet, he leaned forward out of his chair to grab it, but still unsteady on his injured leg, lost his balance and plopped back into his chair. Freya whined and eyed the former Green Beret as he laid the paper on the corner of his desk, still putting it out of reach. "I pissed off the wrong combatants."

"You mean the Al-Shabaab—the Somalia-based Islamist extremist group that is allied to al-Qaeda?" Vince slapped the paper on the desk and slid it over.

"They claimed responsibility for the deadly attack at the Kenyan hotel where I believe you took out a number of those assholes."

"Oh, that? Total coincidence I was there and had my gun, bro."

"You're being modest. I read you personally rescued fifty hostages and took out the combatants." He pointed to the writing on the paper. "The British government successfully kept your identity a secret for a long time but evidently someone leaked it."

"And here we are, mate." Trevor laughed.

"Is that why you live in the United States now?"

"No. My wife got sick and we moved here for advanced medical care." He petted Freya's head and scratched under her chin in silence, without adding to the story.

Vince either knew the ending or was observant enough to fill in the blanks but he didn't pursue the questioning. After a prolonged silence, Trevor offered his own ending to the conversation.

"It was the catch or kill mission of the leader of Boko Haram and I killed him."

"Let me guess. They put out a hit on you?"

"Maybe, but because they kidnapped the dog, I think it's more an act of revenge. The way they think putting a bullet in my head is too easy. They want to inflict the most possible pain."

"You think they planned to collect the ransom and not return the dog?"

"Cover your ears, Freya." Trevor covered the dog's ears. "I think these slimy bastards were hoping to collect the ransom, torture my dog, and return her deceased body as evidence of how brutal they are." He uncovered Freya's ears. "Why I opted for a double cover in finding Freya fast."

"I get it, man, but you need to do a multiplication table on your security. How many people on your personal security detail?"

"I had two but Kacie put them on hiatus for a while when she shot them."

"Your father is a member of the British diplomatic corp. Does that give you security at the house?"

"Not at the house because they're with my father, who is out of the country, but they won't hit me at his house because of that. They don't want the entire British military and the Secret Service coming down on their rank asses. We do have a safe room my father had installed when he first bought the place. It's under the staircase and state of the art. Also, impossible to detect."

"Good on him. What about hiring Kacie as a bodyguard until they're caught? Your review of her work was rave."

Trevor cleared his throat. "She's the reason I'm here in person. I'm very grateful for her mission success." He folded his hands on the desk. "She'd have to relocate to Virginia for an extended period. Would that be a problem for her family or her boyfriend?"

"Neither."

"They wouldn't mind?"

"She doesn't have family here and no boyfriend. Every horny male on my team has already scoped out and verified she's single and from the scuttle butt, not even a little bit available."

"I have no doubt every one of them would like to have a go at her. She's beautiful and a very skilled operator."

Vince eyed Trevor with swinish suspicion. "But not you, my friend, as we frown on fraternizing with clients."

"Only a frown?"

"It's grounds for dismissal, Trevor, so don't bang the help." Trevor sensed a territorial edge to Vince's voice and decided to challenge it.

"So you maintain control over your employee's personal lives as well as professional?" His own anger seeped into his response.

"Emotions can compromise a mission. If anyone understands that, it's you, Trevor."

"I get it, Vince. Hands off but my eyeballs still work."

"Listen, man, she doesn't know about the two dudes you sent to shadow her but I guarantee she won't be happy, and I'm going to tell her."

"Kacie's a total pro. She'll understand once I explain my reasoning."

"I call bullshit. You wanna put money on that?"

Trevor yanked his wallet out of the side pocket of his cargo pants and withdrew a fifty-dollar bill. "You're going to be paying for my dinner tonight, mate," he said as he slapped the bill on the table. His bluster was more hope than certainty. If he was honest with himself, his reaction to being compromised on a mission would be nothing short of ballistic. How could he expect Kacie's reaction to be any different? Still, his desire to see her again outweighed the consequences of being on the receiving end of a pissed off Marine.

"Let's put this bet in play," he said to Vince.

****

Word traveled fast in small military communities and Valor Security was no exception. Kacie's phone started blowing up about three minutes after Trevor walked through the front door. Jacy's text had simply read—*Hubba, hubba.*—

Why was Trevor here, in person? There was nothing about her abrupt exit from his house or, thank goodness, their close encounter in his review of her work. To his credit, he'd kept it professional. Her heart raced as she hurried along the corridor leading to the office next to the main conference room where a convenient one-way mirror had been installed last year. Kacie glanced at her reflection in the window and frowned at her lack of makeup—not even lipstick and her hair in a tight bun at the base of her neck. This was her norm and he'd seen her like this before but suddenly, if awkward was a dress, she was wearing it.

A second text from Jacy showed up and read, — *Boss wants you in the conference room pronto.*—

She inhaled a deep breath but couldn't stop the

welling tightness in her chest.

Kacie replied with a text, —*On my way.*—

She needed control of her emotions before she faced him. A peek, without his knowledge, would give her the edge. Kacie rounded the corner and checked both directions. The hallway was empty. She dropped into a duck walk and hurried toward the next office. As she scooted by the conference room door, Freya whined and the door swung open, knocking her on her ass. Freya pounced on top of her and, with the enthusiasm of greeting an old friend, licked her face. A hand reached down, grabbed her wrist and with too strong a tug landed her pressed against Trevor's chest. His peppermint-tinged breath enveloped her and she closed her eyes for a second before Vince's voice boomed, "What the hell, O'Shea?"

****

"My bad, mate," Trevor said to Vince as he righted Kacie's stance. "Freya acted like she needed a bathroom break." He petted the dog's head. "I swung open the door without looking."

"I'll call one of the staff to take Freya out so we can continue our meeting," Vince said.

With his arms crossed, Vince glanced from Trevor to Kacie with an eyebrow cocked and a skeptical twist to his mouth. "Well, O'Shea, since you're here, c'mon in." He uncrossed his arms and waved her into the boardroom. "Trevor has something he wants to say to you."

The moisture accumulated under his arms as he took a seat. There was no way to soften what he had to say. She would be pissed. Fortunately, Kacie chose a seat on the opposite side and the table was broad enough to prevent her from reaching across to strangle him.

"I'm not going to sugar coat this," he started. "I misjudged your capabilities."

"Because I'm a female?"

"Not at all. Because I've never worked with you before. Believe me, you looked damn good on paper and I trusted Vince's judgement. He glanced at the man sitting like a stone at the head of the table. "Truthfully, I was a bit dodgy in describing the incident as a simple kidnapping."

"I assume you read my brief?" She punched her finger on the report binder positioned in front of her.

He nodded his head.

"Then you read the part where I describe the men I encountered at the barn as professional, most likely military and not juvenile dognappers?"

He hesitated, observing the stillness in her erect body.

"That was a question," she said.

"You're correct. They were military."

"And you know that how?"

"Because I hired them as backup to your mission in case you failed," he said with a sheepish shrug.

The sting of the swat to Trevor's cheek twisted his head. He snapped back, and with eyes locked on hers, he said, "I deserved that."

"I could have killed those two friendlies, you son of a bitch." Kacie squeezed the rolled binder in her hand.

He anticipated another swing and shoved his chair away from the table, barely missing Freya. "But you didn't."

"I witnessed the impact. One was hit in the chest and one in the leg." Her voice rose on a high pitch. "Jesus, Trevor, how could they be okay?"

"They both wore bulletproof vests in case they encountered the kidnappers. The guy you hit in the leg had a flesh wound. No artery. No bone. Full recovery expected."

"I'll bet they're pissed at me and I hope to hell they're pissed at you."

"Not pissed at you and fully compensated with bonuses, so not pissed at me either." He sighed. "Truth is, I didn't expect you to arrive at the barn so quickly. I instructed my men to stand down and not engage unless they encountered the kidnappers. You surprised them." He glanced at Vince, hoping for a buffer or a mediator but the guy propped his cowboy boots on the table and clasped his hands behind his head. *What? Was he enjoying this?*

"I'm sorry, Kacie. You're an excellent operator and I should have trusted you."

"You didn't have to come all the way out here to tell me that. A card would have sufficed." She stood, pushed the chair under the table and walked to the door.

"You leaving?" Vince asked.

"No reason to stay." She paused and faced him, ignoring Trevor.

Vince regarded her with a smug grin, obviously amused by her bravado. "Trevor wants to hire you again. Those bad hombres are still out there and still a threat."

"You have plenty of talented operators here that can do the job." Kacie thrust her shoulders back and lifted her chin. "Pick one."

Without a backward glance, she exited, letting the door slam shut.

Chapter Six

As Kacie hurried down the hallway, Trevor's voice, begging her to wait, only propelled her faster toward the first corner. The last words, "They're after Emma," stung with the force of a hundred angry hornets. She spun on her heel. Heaviness flooded her chest and throttled her attempts to breathe. All efforts to suck in air convulsed the muscles in her rib cage into a tighter squeeze. Triggered, she stopped and, with her eyes closed, rested her back flat against the wall. *Time for box breathing.* Her karate instructor, a retired Navy SEAL and someone who understood the fog of war, taught her the breathing method as a means of handling combat anxiety. She breathed in slowly. *One, two, three, four. Hold. One, two, three, four.*

The click, click, click of Freya's toenails on the tile floor and the thud and drag of Trevor's boots penetrated the concentration of her deep breathing.

A cold nose bumped her bare arm. Aware Freya and probably Trevor had joined her, she continued her meditative process. *Breath out. One, two, three, four.*

Without opening her eyes or changing her stance, she asked, "Is this another one of your subterfuges?"

"I might be an asshole but I'm not *that* big of an asshole."

His hot breath brushed her ear as he whispered his answer. She reached down and rubbed the sweet space on top of Freya's head where the hair lay in a diamond pattern. "That remains to be seen."

"You're free to think whatever you want of me but this is about Emma." He touched her shoulder. "Please, just hear me out."

"Where is Emma right now?" She wouldn't put it past this Brit to have Emma stashed somewhere close so he could bring her out, if necessary, in a crescendo move to close her on the job. Anyone who met Emma would be mesmerized by the little charmer and Trevor understood it.

"She's safe. My father has a secluded cabin in the Shenandoah Mountains that's registered under an untraceable corporate name. My two friends and Annabelle are with her.

"Are you insane?" She kept her voice to a whisper.

"It depends." He hesitated. "Why do you ask?"

"Annabelle." She couldn't believe his thick headedness. "How do you know you can trust her?"

"She's a friend, a good friend, and Emma likes her. I didn't think having two armed military males alone with Emma was a good idea."

"Don't you find it odd the kidnapping occurred at her place of business by members of a violent terrorist group but she didn't have a scratch on her? Not a ding?"

"They weren't after her. Why didn't you mention this suspicion in the briefing?"

"Because I had no solid proof. Only a hunch." Kacie squatted, resting her hands on her thighs. Trevor reached down to help Kacie up but she flashed her hand. "I'm thinking." After a few minutes, she rose and faced him. "I need to ask, not because I give a shit, but for the security of the mission if I choose to accept your offer."

"Fire away."

"Are you romantically involved with Annabelle?"

"Are you kidding me? That's your question?"

"No, I'm not kidding. I saw the fawning gaze and drip, drip, drip of adoration when she talked about you." She raised an eyebrow. "Are you screwing her?"

Trevor's boisterous laughter filled the space. "That's quite a compliment, Kacie."

"It wasn't intended as one." She huffed, realizing her question implied the fawning and adoration came *after* the suggested sex. Heat rose on her neck. "I'm only asking for security reasons. I want to rule her out as a liability."

"The answer is no. Not my type." Trevor stepped closer to Kacie, less than an arm's length away. "I have a question for you, Miss O'Shea."

A scent flooded her senses. He smelled like a deep forest of Christmas trees. She eased into his space, intoxicated by the bouquet. "What's your question?" she asked in a breathy voice.

"From the first day I laid eyes on you, I sensed a connection. Maybe it was wishful thinking but I'm keen to know if you feel it too." With a quick, right-handed sweep, he brushed the sun-streaked blonde strand of wayward hair off his face.

Every physical move he made exuded masculinity and certainty. Tanned from his love of outdoor activities, his face framed deep-blue eyes, which softened when he spoke to Emma or Freya, but grew icy and intense in moments of anger. She peered into their depths and warmth met her gaze. If she admitted to being wildly attracted to him, his response would be lightning quick. Was he aware of the no fraternizing clause in her contract? Maybe his cockiness allowed him the luxury that he could have it both ways. She didn't have that luxury. She needed and wanted this job.

With a gentle shove to his shoulder, she teased, "You're okay."

"Rubbish. You're crazy about me but I accept the challenge of ascending your scale until I reach, 'too hot to ignore.'"

"Knock yourself out, Trevor, but if, and that's a *huge* if, I agree to work for you, there are certain conditions that I'll insist on being met."

She could take the safe route and walk away. The people she worked with were all experienced operators, and any one of them could perform the duties Trevor required. Call it justification but she already had a relationship with the family and held the highest qualifications for protection work. Confident she had the self-discipline to work with Trevor and keep their relationship professional, she'd make her pitch to Vince.

"You'll be in charge one hundred percent," he said. "Pick who you want on the assignment."

"Swear your guys won't try to 'off me' in my sleep and they can stay." She made a cross-your-heart-hope-to-die sign over her chest. "I know you served with them and have their loyalty."

"I swear, respect will ooze out of their pores."

"And here I thought the Brits were so highbrow." She chuckled, then started back toward the conference room with Trevor. "Annabelle needs to vamoose back to her dog grooming, like yesterday." She glanced at Trevor and winked.

"Consider her vamoosed."

"Good man." She gave him a thumbs-up. "Let's find Vince and get this rodeo started."

A challenge had always been her signature desire. It was yet to be determined if she was worthy of this one. No doubt she could keep Emma safe, but what about her heart?

****

Trevor scribbled his signature, barely aware his hand had a pen in it. Vince had agreed to assign Kacie with the addition of a significant bonus termed 'special duty' pay. He'd signed off on Kacie's conditions as well. The colossal cost of safeguarding Emma, his primary objective, wasn't important. What mattered was he'd retained the best protection agent money could buy. He didn't have cash to burn but he'd made a killing on the sale of his countryside English estate and the British government was generous in its compensation for his combat injury. Concerned, his father insisted Emma and he stay at his Virginia home, rent free, where he could receive TLC from Hazel until his leg healed. All in all, a peachy set-up. One he appreciated.

"We're all done here," Vince said, setting his pen on the table.

The penetrating tone jarred Trevor to the present. He glanced at the Marine sitting across the table and sucked in a breath. She'd been clear about the limits of their relationship as long as she was employed by Valor but she hadn't specified it as one of her written conditions. Did she assume he knew and agreed? Or was it a clever way to leave the door open, if only a crack?

"Trevor, care to join us for dinner?" Vince collected the papers they'd signed and slipped them in a binder. "I'm treating the crew to barbecue at a little joint downtown."

Trevor glanced at Kacie hoping for a sign of encouragement but was met with a noncommittal expression. He checked his watch.

"When's your flight home?" Kacie asked.

"First flight tomorrow morning." He rubbed Freya's head. "Don't want to keep my lady out too late. I should head for the hotel and pack it in, but thanks for the invite."

"Freya, are you a party pooper?" Kacie kneeled and scratched the dog's chest.

"Ruff." Freya barked.

"I distinctly heard her say she loves barbecue." Kacie accepted Trevor's hand helping her up. "Don't be stuffy. Join us. You'll be right at home with these guys."

"Right." He nodded. "I can sleep on the plane."

"Leave your rental here and ride with me," Vince said.

Disappointed Kacie didn't make a counteroffer, Trevor waved her through the door and swung in behind Vince. It was for the best. Any time alone with Kacie, amped up his desire and conflicted his priorities. Once the threat got neutralized, all bets were off.

Chapter Seven

Kacie checked the GPS on her dial. Only a few more hours on the interstate before she exited and drove the windy, narrow road to Marlowe senior's cabin. Driving had been her idea for security reasons and the monotony of interstate travel helped her think. Only Trevor, Vince, and Crockett had her itinerary. At her instruction, Trevor sent Annabelle home. She didn't care what excuse he used because if left to her there'd be a boot mark on the woman's butt. A niggle in her gut said the dog groomer wasn't trustworthy.

She checked the GPS again in anticipation of the drive through the Shenandoah mountains with Fall plummeting the Virginia landscape into brilliant hues of red and gold. The temperatures at night turned crisp and the days, although shorter, defined perfect outdoor weather. But the season change reminded her of the coming winter. The cabin, although remote, would isolate them from rescue if needed and didn't have a safe room. Unfair to Emma, she'd be denied all the community activities she enjoyed. Kacie planned to get a preliminary sitrep from the two men currently watching the cabin and from Trevor about any red flags, but her inclination was to relocate Emma back to the father's McLean house. The idea Trevor conveyed that Emma was a target had not panned out in any real sense. Things had been quiet.

The Heart of Valor

The final few hours flew by as she mentally prepared for her new assignment and seeing Trevor again. Their recent communication had been cordial but entirely professional. She'd experienced a different side of Trevor at dinner with the team. One she enjoyed. The other veterans showered him with respect as he shared war stories with a light-hearted pizazz and sense of humor. His exploits had made the news but the media wasn't privy to everything. She liked the fact he felt comfortable enough with her group to share the details and how he'd glanced at her as if to measure her response.

GPS directions ended and Trevor's written directions brought her up a steep, forested hill. The stone and log cabin perched at the top stood as a testament to the British way of downplaying. Trevor had simply described it as a rustic cabin with a wood-burning stove which served as a weekend getaway. She parked her car in the circular gravel driveway and peered through her front window in awe. *Holy Cow.* The two-story house was an architectural vision with a wide wraparound porch and a large deck that extended from the side where she assumed the kitchen was located. There was a double chimney for a fireplace. She stepped out of her car. Two buff, twenty something men lounging on the porch waved. The bulge in their jackets indicated they were packing heat. She returned the wave. The front screen door slammed against the wall. Freya bounded out to greet her followed by Emma and Trevor.

"Nice digs," she called, bracing her stance in preparation for the eighty-pound canine's welcome. *You look amazing in your red flannel shirt with the sleeves rolled up over your bulging forearms.* With one eye on Trevor and Emma, Kacie's peripheral vision caught Freya's approach, but rather than resist the impact, she leaned into the dog's u-shaped tail wags. Down on her knees, she hugged and petted Freya's head and body, gently controlling her until Trevor commanded her to heel.

"Kacie, you took too long." Emma's welcome was between a giggle and a scream.

"Thanks, I think," Kacie replied as she stood. The little munchkin, cuter than ever if that was possible, wore a bright red hoodie and matching flowered tights with fur-topped boots. Someone had parted her fine hair into two bunches and fastened them with rubber bands on top of her head. The little girl was styling.

"How was your trip?" Trevor, now within arm's reach, refrained from an embrace and instead stuffed his hands in his pants pockets.

"Uneventful, just like I like it." She skimmed his face. "How are things here?" She glanced at the two men in dark sunglasses still on the porch. "We good?"

Trevor, sharp as a knife's edge, laughed, then waved them over.

"I promise I don't bite," she said as she extended her right hand to the first male who approached. His brutal grip was probably payback. She held her smile and refused to wince. "Looking forward to working with you."

"Likewise. Name's Joey. This is Sam." He nodded toward the second, younger guy who walked up with a slight limp as Joey stepped to the side.

"No hard feelings, ma'am," he said with a noticeable Southern accent.

"None intended." She glanced at Trevor. "You're American?" Surprised Trevor chose an American veteran for security when he had plenty of British special forces contacts, she assumed he had his reasons.

"Ma'am, if I might add, it was dark at the barn and difficult to observe how beautiful you are. If I'd known, I would've surrendered." Dimples accented the impossibly handsome face as the soldier's grin spread. No doubt he had shmoozed his way into many panties.

Trevor jangled the coins, or was it keys, in his pockets and studied the ground. Freya sat riveted next to him, eyes focused and intent on her master. *Classic trained reaction for a service dog who senses unease in their charge. Or was the dog picking up on her discomfort?*

"I think you're pretty too." Emma clasped her hand and, with a toothy smile, melted Kacie's embarrassment.

Kacie stooped over and cupped Emma's chin. "Thanks for having my back, little one." She doubted a six-year-old would understand the term, but despite the short time they'd known each other, a bond had developed.

"Thanks, soldier," she said to Sam. In an unspoken but understood message, she used her two fingers and indicated she'd be keeping an eye on him by pointing from her eyes to him.

"Heard and understood," Joey said as he dragged Sam toward the porch.

"Let's get you settled in," said Trevor. "Need help with your things?"

"Sure." Still by her car, she pressed the rear latch. "If you could grab my duffle bag, I'll get my rifle and gun cases."

"What can I carry? asked Emma, looking expectedly at the two adults.

"How about my purse? It's heavy but I know you can handle it."

Emma raised her arm and flexed her bicep. Kacie slung the shoulder strap over the little girl's arm. Then, stepped back, crossed her arms, and nodded in approval. She engaged Trevor in lighthearted conversation, fully aware the two guys were evaluating her as they headed up the gravel path. After a slight nod to Joey and Sam, she stepped on the porch. Trevor placed his hand in the small of her back and ushered her in the front door. She thought she heard Sam say, "Noted."

****

Trevor stacked logs next to the wood-burning stove with a light-hearted toss. Different from his usual meticulous assembly, Kacie's presence lifted his mood and shifted his priorities. He hummed a familiar tune, "My Money's On You", when only a few months ago he'd been humming, "Just Ask The Lonely." If he could dance, he'd probably moonwalk across the floor.

"You're in a good mood," Kacie said as she entered the room, holding a mug of steaming liquid. Freya wagged her tail but remained at his side.

"I'm glad you're here." He lifted his head and smiled. "I see you found the hot chocolate."

"Emma offered to share."

"You must rate." He raised his eyebrows. "But the real test is did she give up any marshmallows?"

"Two, as a matter of fact." She pointed to the contents in her cup, then took a sip. "So good." She smacked her lips.

Trevor paused and smiled. Their banter flowed in a natural exchange. He'd like to pretend she wasn't here as a hired professional. A nice hot toddy by the fire or a midnight star-gazing walk would be his preference. He'd caught her glancing at him when she didn't think he noticed. The attraction was mutual, but her contract was proving to be a real cockblocker.

"We need to talk."

"Sure," she said and closed the distance until their shoulders touched. "What's up?"

"As you suggested, I sent Annabelle home but she wasn't happy. Her protest seemed over the top to me so I ran a background check on her."

"Good move. Any red flags?"

"One. She was associated with a radical group in college with ties to several anarchist leaders from guess which country?"

"Kenya."

"Bingo." He snorted.

"Any indication she's still connected?"

"Not that I could find."

"This doesn't change anything, Trevor."

"She knows the location of the cabin." He kicked one of the logs. "I led her right to us."

"True but I think her protest in being shunted home has more to do with her personal interest in you than a desire to harm Emma." She grabbed his hand. "I was planning to recommend, insist actually, we relocate back to your father's residence in Virginia."

"You're...putting...a bull's eye... on my daughter's...back." He kept his voice low but his words measured.

"She's safer, we all are, hiding in plain sight. Out here, our team, although good, is all we have. As far as we know, there are only two enemy combatants who couldn't even pull off a successful dog knapping." She huffed, then continued. "You haven't received any new threats, correct?"

"Right. It's been quiet but they haven't been arrested." He rubbed his palms up his face. "I hired you for your expertise in personal security. If you can guard an overseas embassy, I feel confident you can keep us safe."

"I appreciate the vote of confidence. We'll spend the night here and travel in a convoy back to Virginia tomorrow." She squeezed his hand and let go. "I'd like the guys to stay on the team for now."

"Oh, I know one horny, young Army dude who won't object."

"You have nothing to worry about, Mr. Marlowe." She regarded him with a quizzical expression.

With a sudden tug, he pulled her into his chest and breathed in her feminine scent. His heart celebrated her closeness. She lifted her chin and gazed at him with parted lips. It was all the invitation he needed. He kissed her with unleashed passion, slipping his tongue past her lips, savoring the trace of chocolate on her tongue as he explored her mouth. She surrendered to his embrace, then stiffened and retreated.

"What I was about to say was," she sighed, pressing on his chest, "you have nothing to worry about because of my fraternizing clause. This," —she pointed to him and then herself—"a hard no."

Time has a way of breaking barriers down and I'm a patient man. "Right then. No fraternizing."

"There's a reason the clause is in there," she said.

"I understand. You need mission focus and repeated, hot sex with this," —he swept his hand down his body— "disregard the bum leg, would be a distraction."

Kacie held her sides, laughing. Humor had been his intention. He wanted to keep the mood light and if there was no potential for romance right now.... "Laughing at a cripple now, are we?"

His comment only made her laugh again while stuttering, "No, no, not laughing at your injury."

"My American accent, then?"

"Stop." She playfully punched him in the gut. "I'm going to pee myself."

The image of her pants down around her ankles danced around in his head and with it an erection grew. His commando style of not wearing underwear magnified his bulge. Desperate to adjust himself without Kacie noticing, he feigned dropping his cane. She automatically bent to retrieve it. With her head bowed, he clutched and shifted his package.

"Feel better?" she asked as she stood upright, and with a wink, handed him his cane.

Chapter Eight

Trevor rode back to Virginia with Freya and Sam, declining her invitation with the lame excuse Sam and he needed to discuss schedules. His boner was a pleasant surprise, at least for her. More of a surprise for him. Emma had wandered in, requesting her bedtime story shortly after their encounter. She turned in after they went upstairs but sleep evaded her. The chemistry between them was undeniable, but so was her contract with Valor Securities. She could quit and get an administrative job with some faceless corporation or teach karate in a dojo, which would leave her free to pursue a relationship with Trevor, but while one void would be filled, another would be created. Working with other veterans who had experienced similar combat stresses served her well. She'd landed her dream job in a safe space with common ground and no drama where she was trusted implicitly. There was no doubt in her mind, under different circumstances, she'd ensure Trevor had at least one daily boner. He'd already kicked her hormones into overdrive.

Kacie slowed as the posted speed limit reduced and retrieved a crinkled photo from the visor. Worn from use, she waited until the first stop light off the beltway and viewed it until the light changed. Three members of her team lost in a ferocious firefight while engaged with the enemy. She attended all their funerals and looked into the vacant eyes of their grieving widows as she handed each one of them a folded American flag. Confused and angry that she'd survived the ambush when they had not, she returned home, broken. Kacie blamed herself, although she'd been cleared of any dereliction of duty by intelligence officers who viewed the body cams of her unit. They determined she had performed her duties as overwatch in an exemplary manner despite a hidden suicide bomber. They would have listed her as one of the casualties had she been in the alley with her team and not ordered to perform overwatch.

A horn behind her blew and she waved. Joe pulled up in the lane beside her and indicated she roll down her window.

"Hey, you sat through a green light. Everything okay?"

"Yeah." She noticed Emma's curious stare and wiggled her fingers in a reassuring wave. "A little tired but I'm good." She rolled up the window and stuffed the picture back under the visor. When the light turned green, she waited for Joe to pass her and pulled in behind him.

****

Hazel stood on the front doorstep wringing her hands. Trevor, in the lead car, spotted her first as they turned the corner onto Falstaff Road. He punched Sam in the arm and pointed to his distraught housekeeper. Sam sped up, reaching the driveway a few minutes before the other cars. She waved a brief acknowledgement and hurried down the steps to Trevor's window.

"What's the matter, Hazel?"

"I'm afraid we have some bad news."

"A new threat?" Trevor spun his head around in both directions, checking the outside perimeter while Sam pulled his gun from the glove box. "Did you call the cops?"

"No, my boy." She visually searched the street. "Where's Kacie?"

"She's a few minutes behind us, pulling up the rear behind Joe and Emma." He swung open the car door and stepped out. "From the look on your face, this is bad. Why didn't you call me?"

"It's news best delivered in person and probably by you."

"Jesus. What is it?"

"Her employer, Mr. Samuels, phoned yesterday and asked that I relay the message directly to you, in person." She wiped her hands on her apron and continued. "Her friend, Mr. Crockett, has been killed in a robbery gone wrong."

"Bugger." Trevor slapped his hands on top of his head. This was truly horrific news. He'd met Davy at the company dinner and observed Kacie's adoration for her former superior. At first handshake, when Davy glared at him with a measured gaze, he'd thought they had a romantic relationship. He figured the reaction was based on jealousy but as the night progressed, he realized it was platonic and very close. The kind of friendship forged from trust gained in battle. A once in a lifetime friendship that would be devastating to lose.

"So Crockett got robbed?" Trevor's gaze was now fixed on the street as a car slowed in front of the house. Kacie had arrived and was about to get hit with a metaphorical sledgehammer.

"Apparently Mr. Crockett stepped in to prevent a robbery at a convenience store. He disarmed one of the assailants but a second one shot him in the back and fled." She whispered more of the data from Vince.

Trevor winced. His mind raced with how to broach the news. Certainly not in front of a crowd. Kacie was already out of her car, headed straight for him. He signaled Sam to vamoose with Joe. Sam exited the car with a casual wave to Kacie as he passed and waited on the corner for Joe, who would need to be filled in without Emma hearing. His daughter's capacity for empathy far exceeded her tender age. Her attachment to Kacie made her especially vulnerable. She'd already lived one too many days like this.

"Hazel, please take Freya and Emma inside and keep my nosy little girl busy until after dinner," he whispered.

"Certainly, sir."

Kacie's bright smile faltered as she neared him. He was sure she sensed something wrong when Hazel hunched over and hurried past her, failing to make eye contact.

He clasped his hands behind his back and glanced over her shoulder to confirm no one was within earshot. The team had made themselves invisible. Hazel herded Emma into the house and disappeared.

Trevor would rather bathe in boiling pig grease than witness the emotional meltdown about to occur. He scanned Kacie's expectant expression soon to be replaced by the twist of pain. What heartless bastard would inflict this magnitude of hurt on someone he loved? Yes, if he was honest with himself, the pull she had on him wasn't simply physical, although her beauty was undeniable. The realization that love was no longer an abstract four-letter word found only on a shelf in a dictionary shook him. He thought his ability to be vulnerable with a woman died with his wife but his interest in Kacie exceeded the superficial bounds of employer-employee, even friend. Their core values and beliefs were the same. *I must be the one to tell her.*

"What's wrong?" Kacie asked, her eyes clouded with fear.

Trevor grabbed her forearms and guided her toward the porch steps. His thumbs fidgeted back and forth. *How the hell do I break this to her?*

"What's going on?" she asked.

He opened his hand in a nonverbal invitation to sit on the steps, but she ignored his request.

"Sweetheart, there's been an accident." He hesitated for a few seconds.

"Who?"

"It's Crockett."

Her knees buckled. Trevor helped her onto the first step then joined her with his thigh and shoulder pressed against her for comfort. He wrapped his arm around her and she leaned into his chest.

"How bad?" she whispered.

He hadn't pulled the trigger that ended the Marine Seargent's life, but he might as well have put the gun to Crockett's head. Her eyes held a glimmer of hope and he was about to torch it. This wasn't the first time Trevor had to relay the kind of news that sucked so bad it would forever change a person's life. He braced himself.

"He lost his life saving others in a robbery gone wrong."

"No! No, no, no," She cried out and cupped her palms over her ears.

"Kacie." He reached to hug her, but she pounded her fists into his chest. His breath caught from the impact but didn't try to stop her. He'd do anything to help her deal with the pain.

"Oh God. Not Davy." She whipped her head back and forth. "How could this happen?" Her gaze lifted toward the sky.

Trevor understood she wasn't asking him that question, so he remained silent.

"When?" She returned her gaze to him.

"Earlier this week."

"Why am I just now finding out?" She clenched her fists.

"The police had to investigate and when they went through his belongings, they found a photo of you with Davy clipped to Vince's business card. Vince wanted you to hear the news in person."

"Did he suffer?" She choked back sobs.

"I'll tell you everything I know."

****

Kacie prided herself on having served as a Marine. She worked hard to exemplify the toughness associated with that cadre of men and women. The news about her dearest friend being murdered stripped her defenses to the marrow. She hunched over, choking down a sob.

"I'm sorry." She swiped at the tears persisting down her cheeks.

Trevor lifted her chin. "For what? Caring deeply for a bright light snuffed out for no reason?"

"For pounding on you." She vigorously rubbed her arms. "Kinda chilly when the sun goes down."

"I'm a big boy. I can handle the drubbing." He removed his jacket and draped it over her shoulders. "Better?"

"Yes, thanks." With a light touch to his hand, she continued. "He taught me how to be a warrior. How to survive the chaos of war. How to live with honor and dignity." She gazed into the distance, then forced a smile.

"From what I can see, he was a great teacher."

Kacie shivered and pulled the jacket tighter around her shoulders. She glanced around and realized they were alone outside. The guys along with Hazel, Emma and Freya had disappeared, but someone turned on the porch light. Were they all in the house, peeking through the curtains, witnesses to her misery? A flush crept across her cheeks.

"Does everyone know?"

"Just Hazel, but I assure you both men would be in your corner. Sam and Joe are combat veterans and no strangers to the loss of a close battle buddy."

Hazel? "How did Hazel find out?"

"Vince called her with the news. He figured she'd be the easiest person to contact and would be the one person who knew where we could be reached. He thought it best the news be delivered in person." He smiled. "I volunteered."

"Thank you." She rubbed the heel of her right palm against her chest. "It hurts."

"Your chest?" His brow furrowed into deep lines.

"No, my heart." Kacie's breath caught as she tried to prevent the renewed flow of tears but sadness claimed her like a vulture snagging the last bite of carrion. Her shoulders shook with sobs she couldn't tamp down. The chill of the night pierced the nylon material of the jacket loose around her shoulders and a shiver erupted along her spine.

Davy, whoever made you suffer has no future. I'm coming for the son of a bitch who took you from me.

She wasn't sure if she announced her threat out loud, but Trevor, who had been quietly solemn next to her, enfolded her in his arms. Waves of warmth flowed through her tired, cold body as he rocked her. He kissed the top of her head and whispered, "I'm here. Whatever you need, I'm here."

Trevor continued to rock her until the sobs subsided. She breathed deep breaths, gaining control of her emotions and rested her head on Trevor's rock-hard chest.

"The angels have him now." She sighed, then added pointing to her chest, "but the Grim Reaper is coming for his killer."

"The cops caught his killer," said Trevor. "He'll never see the light of day again."

"What if he gets some fancy bullshit lawyer who gets him off or gets a reduced sentence?"

"Already taken care of."

There was a sinister gleam in Trevor's eyes. She withdrew from his embrace and stood. A moment of intuitive understanding transmitted between them before Trevor spoke again.

"It's all about timing and this fucker's is bad. The Deputy Sheriff was transporting him from the local jail to the Denver courthouse the next day when a freak landslide took out the van and rolled it over a precipice. The driver jumped just in time before the first boulders plunged down the hill. But as karma would have it, he didn't have time to release the prisoner from his shackles."

Kacie nodded her head. "Emma must be wondering where her dad is. We should go inside." She stuck her arm inside his and they walked up the steps together.

Chapter Nine

Kacie excused herself from dinner and went straight to her bedroom. After a chorus of no apologies necessary, Hazel offered to bring dinner to her room. If she had to pick a location to be when she received soul-shattering news, the Marlowe residence was perfect. Even sweet Emma embraced her with a wordless hug before she ascended the stairs.

Tiredness engulfed her body. With each step up another stair, the weight in her legs grew heavier. The banister served as a much-needed aid to pull her forward and prevent her from falling backward. Her vision blurred. She paused to regain her bearings and overheard Trevor on the phone with someone describing her current state as all over the emotional scale and vulnerable. He thought it best for her to remain here for a few days before flying home for the funeral. She guessed Trevor was talking to Vince as he communicated current threat level nominal. No replacement necessary. A tiny glimmer of hope kept her from blacking out when he ended the conversation with "Yes, she's phenomenal and deserves a leadership role in your organization." Well, at least she wasn't getting fired for falling apart on the job.

Sleep eluded her. Kacie tossed the covers back and checked the clock. Two thirty a.m. *UGH. A good night's rest is what I need before I tackle the phone calls, my flight back to Denver and the funeral arrangements for Davy.* She swung her legs onto the floor and shuffled toward the bathroom, eyeballing the medicine cabinet. The dim night light threw a shadow over the puffy eyes and makeup smears on her face but when she flipped the main switch and caught a glimpse of herself, she grunted. *Good Lord. I'm a mess.*

She blew the random strand of hair off her face and rummaged through the cabinet but there were only the usual first aid supplies and dental floss. No sleep meds. Hadn't Trevor ever heard of Ambien?

Convinced Hazel would have a supply downstairs, she tossed a t-shirt over her head and stepped toward the bedroom door but stopped. The house was eerily quiet, with only dim, ambient light. Could she be anymore alone? The thought she'd never see Mark Davis Crockett again or hear his deep laugh was a gut punch. Her breathing became labored as she struggled to suppress the memories. She kicked the wall, hoping the pain would override the images of a brilliant, dark-skinned man who served as a lighthouse in her life, guiding her safely to shore through stormy seas.

With her palm flat against the wall, Kacie felt her way down the hall to Trevor's room and found his door opened a crack. She slipped in the room and gazed at him sleeping for a few seconds under the glow of a rock salt lamp before closing the door and locking it. The comfort of his arms was what she needed most, and she was willing to pay the price for her indiscretion. As she neared the bed, he pulled back the covers, revealing his naked body. She yanked off her t-shirt, slid in beside him until the warmth of his skin found hers, and lightly kissed him on the lips.

"Are you sure about this?" he asked.

"I don't want to be alone." Unable to muster the reply she wanted to give, she wrapped her arms around his neck and kissed him again, harder this time, a full court press.

"I think you know how much I want you but if comfort is all you're looking for, we can sleep. I need to hear you say you want us."

Her nipples tightened and the ache high in her vagina spread down her thighs. The pounding in her chest replaced the hollow thud. "I want all of you." She grabbed his hand and inserted it between her legs. "Now."

****

Her dark eyes telegraphed desire. He'd imagined this moment and mentally choreographed each move. His goal of giving her carnal pleasure spiraled his own need into a rock-hard erection. He cupped her chin and leaned in for a kiss, finding her lips parted enough for his tongue to slide inside. Hers was waiting, eager and hungry. His palm caressed her pubic mound, initiating her moaned, "Yes, yes."

Trevor fought to maintain control as the single-minded drive to empty himself inside her dueled with the knowledge she came to him in a vulnerable state. He removed his hand and broke off the kiss. A couple of deep breaths regulated his jagged breathing so he could speak.

"I want you also and have since day one." He brushed the over-the-eyebrow bangs off her forehead, admiring the golden shine. "But I'd like to take it slow."

"Why?" She propped up on her elbow.

"In case you change your mind."

"You think this is sympathy sex?" Her voice rose in frustration.

"No. I, well, I don't want it to be."

"Make good love to me, buddy, slow, fast, hard is best but…."

Those words of affirmation were all Trevor needed. With a tug, he rolled her on top of him. She wasted no time and straddled his hips, offering a perfect view of her more-than-a-handful, breasts. Before he could act, she satisfied his need to fondle them by directing his palms across her nipples and dark pink areola. With his eyes closed, he massaged every inch and listened to her breathing grow heavier. She caught one of his hands and directed it to her bottom. He started by caressing the muscle but strengthened the touch to kneading when she started to rock back and forth. Her head tilted back, and she stroked her flushed throat, letting her hand caress a path down her body to his hard shaft. He'd exceeded his limit on restraint and craved to be inside her. He groaned as she sank down the full length of his member. With his one leg out of commission, he used his other leg to brace himself as she pumped slow at first than increased the intensity until her breasts bounced in a rhythmic dance. He held on to her waist while keeping eye contact until she thrust herself forward, shuttering in ecstasy. The pent-up need in him exploded and unleashed weeks of longing to make love to Kacie.

"Sweet," she purred. "Uh, You're the best." She crumpled in a pile on his chest.

He rubbed her back with his finger, moving in circular patterns. A fulfilling relaxation spread through his body to his extremities.

"Blinding," Trevor said. "Perfectly blinding."

Kacie raised up on her elbows and viewed him with narrowed eyes.

"Are you disappointed?"

"No, baby. Not at all." He chuckled. "Just the opposite."

"Translate, please." She rolled off him and propped up on her side.

"That's British for excellent or superb."

"That's more like it, mister." She punched her index finger into his chest.

Her feigned indignation was almost British in its humor. Curious how since he'd moved to America, he'd given effort to extinguish his British habits and expressions, adopting a more American view, while Kacie endeavored to at least understand British traditions. Her profession was serious in nature, and she projected the demeanor in heaps. He reveled in her light banter and jabs at him.

"Since neither of us smoke, do you want something to eat or drink?" he asked with a chortle, then checked the clock on the bedside table. Four a.m. He pointed to the clock. "Or we could sleep?"

"When does Hazel get up? She looks like an early riser to me."

"It never varies. Up at six a.m. Reliable as Big Ben." He glanced at her. "That's the—"

"I know what Big Ben is, silly." She punched his arm. "Two whole hours? How about seconds?" She waggled her eyebrows.

Except for a kill order from a terrorist leader hanging over his head, worry was in the rearview. Kacie was on his team and in his bed.

Chapter Ten

Conflicted was an understatement. Last night proved there was a genuine connection between them and not simply a physical attraction. Trevor's concern for her well-being was evident. Now what?

Kacie realized she'd have to come clean with Vince at some point. Although there were no new credible threats against Trevor, her gut told her something was simmering out there. Of all the operators at Valor Security, she had the most experience with this type of radical threat as well as firsthand dealings with Boko Haram and their brazen acts of razing entire villages, destroying homes, and displacing the native inhabitants. No doubt, a nasty bunch of villains.

She rolled out of bed and tossed on a t-shirt long enough to hide her weapon, followed by a pair of faded jeans and brown work boots. Emma's chatter and giggles downstairs indicated everyone was awake, which signaled she was on duty. It also reminded her why she wanted to see this job through. Trevor was a seasoned operator, but Emma was innocent. She needed protection.

The two guys had split the night shift while she shared Trevor's bed. They'd be waiting to change over the guard. She checked herself in the mirror in the hallway before descending the stairs. *Does my face have that well-fucked look? Is there a satisfied swagger in my walk?*

She turned the corner into the dining room and was confronted by a full house. Trevor's eyes were locked on her. So were Sam's but, not wanting to seem obvious, checked his watch in an overplayed manner.

"Late night, Kacie?" Sam said tongue-in-cheek.

"Yes, as a matter of fact." She squared her shoulders. "How about you and Joey? Anything to report?" She imagined him saying, "Yes, there was unusual activity in Trevor's room, so we investigated and found you naked on top of him."

"Just the usual nightly noises," he said with a wink.

She glanced at Trevor, who stirred his tea with vigor while trying to maintain a casual demeanor. He rubbed Freya's ears and avoided eye contact with Sam.

Hazel came out of the kitchen and offered her a hot cup of coffee and a plate of eggs. "How'd you sleep last night, dear?"

OMG. Do I have 'great sex' written all over my face? I didn't sleep much because I was having the best sex of my life with your boss. "Fine, Hazel. I slept enough." An unexpected yawn gave her away.

"I'll make a fresh pot of coffee, dear." She hustled into the kitchen.

Kacie thought she heard Hazel utter, 'tsk, tsk' as she pushed through the swinging kitchen door.

"Have a seat and eat your food before it gets cold," Trevor said, patting the chair next to him. "You need your strength." He gazed at her with an endearing smile.

"We'll be in our quarters if you need us," said Joey as he slid his chair back.

"Yeah, we actually sleep when we're off duty." Sam grinned.

"Guys. Enough." Kacie raised both her hands at full stop. "Now shoo. Find someone else to torment." She waved her hands before grabbing her fork and shoveling down the two scrambled eggs.

"Those mates have been with me in more firefights than I care to count. They work for me, not Valor, so our secret stays between us." Trevor laid his hand on her thigh. "Their ribbing is a way of showing you they consider you their equal. No harm intended."

"No harm perceived." She glanced at his hand gripping her thigh. "I did a bad thing, Trevor."

"Before you beat yourself up too much, I want you to know last night meant something to me. The sex was mind blowing but it only confirmed the connection I feel with you. Believe it or not, honest, intimate communication is what I crave. I suppressed my loneliness since my wife died and used work as a substitute. I decided a remedy wasn't possible until I met you. I want more than a one-night stand."

Kacie's heart ached. Her night with Trevor had temporarily relieved her grief and loss over Crockett's death. But duty always came first. Until now.

"What's going on in that pretty head of yours?" He leaned forward.

"When I accepted this assignment, I thought it was a straightforward protection job." She brushed his cheek. "I never imagined you or this."

"So, you feel the same way?"

"Kacie, you're awake." Emma skittered into the room, delight on her face. Her red ringlets were tied up in two heaps on top of her head and her deep blue eyes twinkled. "Lookee what Hazel did?" She splayed her fingernails displaying red color.

"I see. How lovely." Kacie tickled her stomach. "Just like you."

"She could paint yours too." Emma frowned at Kacie's colorless nails.

"Okay. Maybe later."

"That's what Daddy always says." She stuck her fists on her hips. In typical six-year-old fashion she abruptly changed subjects.

"Daddy's leg hurts today. He said he banged it up last night."

"Oh no." Kacie glared at Trevor. "He didn't tell me. How about you get the pain salve, and I'll rub it on his leg."

"Okay." She nodded until the knobs on her head resembled a slinky and ran for the stairs.

"Trevor Marlowe." She stared at his swollen leg. "We'll need to curtail your extracurricular activities."

"Not a chance." He caressed her bosom.

She swiped at his hand. "Hazel could walk in at any minute."

"Raincheck?"

The big question. Was she going to continue violating her agreement to pursue an affair that could compromise her focus and ultimately her mission? On the other hand, Trevor checked all the boxes for her ideal man. If she didn't see where this relationship could go, would she regret the decision for the rest of her life?

****

Kacie never answered his question about their future, but Trevor didn't know if it was because Emma had interrupted them, or she intentionally avoided a response. The need to know compelled him to persist. He'd have to get her alone.

"Hey, Kacie, would you drive me to my eye doctor appointment this afternoon?" He pointed to his sunglasses. "I'm still not cleared to drive."

"Sure, but the guys are more familiar with this area than I am and probably better handling the atrocious traffic and even worse drivers."

Her resume said she's completed special forces courses on urban tactical driving. She's an ace driver. *I have a hunch she's avoiding being alone with me.*

"I have the lads installing some perimeter cameras today. I'd appreciate you taking on this task." He shoved his hands in his pockets. "I could take a cab but I still need security until I'm back to battery." He jiggled the change in his pocket. "Shouldn't be much longer before my vision is back to normal."

"I'm happy to drive you. When is the appointment?" She grabbed her booklet from her back pocket.

"We need to leave in twenty minutes to make it there by two."

"Oh, geez." She shoved the booklet back into her pocket and checked her watch. "Let me review the home security and alert the guys. Meet you back here in twenty."

Exactly twenty minutes later, she hustled around the corner to the front door, car keys dangling from her hand, every hair in place, exuding the demeanor of a total professional. The walls were up and taking them down would be like chipping away at an ice sculpture, one flake at a time.

He concentrated on what they had in common—the military. They compared British Army bootcamp to the United States Marine bootcamp. Kacie proved herself as an official badass. She relayed the stories of her thirteen-week program with humor, although he understood the fifty-four-hour day and night test of endurance known as the Crucible was no laughing matter and a defining experience. He gazed at her as she drove. He wanted to ask her why she left. She didn't have any apparent physical injuries. What happened on her last tour? Overseas operations challenged even the boldest soldier. He experienced that firsthand.

They arrived at the doctor's appointment on time. Kacie had made sure of that. One of the many things he liked about her.

He decided not to pursue how she viewed their relationship for now. He valued their time together and didn't want to do anything to disrupt the flow. Kacie and Freya sat in the waiting room after she insisted on checking out the entire office. Having someone else assure his safety made him feel like a shell of a man. After pressing the doctor for a release, he obtained a partial with the promise a full release would be forthcoming. He still couldn't drive, but the special glasses were no longer required.

"I thought you looked sexy in those shades," Kacie said, after hearing the good news.

"Oh yeah?" He picked them out of his pocket and waved them around. "What about without?"

"Even better." She harnessed Freya in the back seat before entering the driver side of the car.

"Thanks for coming with me." Trevor grabbed her

hand and squeezed. The news about his vision elated his mood. "I think you're accelerating my healing process."

"No extra charge." She laughed.

The day had been perfect—a slice of happiness he didn't want to spoil—but he had to know. He'd often been told he could be abrasive, brusque and confrontational, but he found the best way to handle any problem was head on. She was tough and had shown she could handle him but her emotions were currently delicate. *I'm going with easy does it.*

"You never answered my question."

"What question?"

"Do you want more with me than a one-night stand?"

Kacie's gaze lingered on the rearview mirror for a few seconds before she checked the side mirror. With a sudden swerve, she moved into the passing lane and accelerated.

"What's going on?"

"We're being tailed." She shifted, driving with her left hand, retrieved her weapon from her shoulder holster, and placed it on the console. "Can you shoot with that bad arm?"

"I can shoot blindfolded."

"Good to know. Grab my gun and hold on."

Kacie whipped in and out of traffic at a speed that showed complete confidence. She flicked her gaze between the sideview and rearview mirrors, all the while keeping a sharp watch on the road ahead. Trevor swiveled his head to catch a glance of who was following them. A white paneled van appeared to be tracking their movement.

"White van?"

"Yep."

"They're falling behind."

"Good. I don't want to have a firefight on the beltway."

"Take the next exit. I know a shortcut home."

"Call the team. Tell them we're coming in hot."

Trevor phoned Sam and advised them of the situation. They'd have Emma and Hazel tucked away and be ready for a fight if the culprits were stupid enough to drive into the kill zone.

Chapter Eleven

Kacie and Trevor arrived home with no one in pursuit and no active threat. The men converged in Trevor's office to debrief. Later, they'd convene to formulate any required tactical revisions. They'd also decide if the strategy they were currently running under needed to be adjusted. Relieved, Kacie excused herself and escaped to her bedroom. Vince had texted her earlier, asking how she was doing after the news. Trevor must have told him about her total meltdown. She responded she was okay and would stop in when she returned for the funeral. He also told her Davy's family had been notified of his tragic death and they expected her to reach out. His parents were elderly and she knew they'd be devastated by the loss. She wouldn't add to their grief. He had one younger sister who she'd met once. A lot like Davy, the sister would be the one in charge of the funeral arrangements. She braced herself for the upcoming phone call to Davy's sister about his funeral arrangements.

A light tap on the door startled her. She chose to ignore it and plopped on the bed, phone in hand.

"I know you're in there," Trevor said. "I'm here if you need me."

Maybe she shouldn't go it alone this time. Maybe a broad shoulder to lean on wasn't a sign of weakness. She hated the thought of leaving Trevor and Emma while the possibility of an incident loomed. What if she brought them with her? What if either Sam or Joe came along as well?

"I'm coming." She hopped off the bed and hurried toward the door. When she flung it open, Trevor embraced her.

"Find out when the funeral is. I'm coming with you." He whispered in her ear.

"What about Emma?"

"The guys are good with staying here and keeping her safe. Besides, I'm the target and I have the best protection in the business."

She started to object but he kissed her while backstepping her into the bedroom and kicking the door shut behind him.

****

To say she handled adversity well would be an understatement. Trevor held Kacie's hand while she listened to Davis Crocket's sister on the dreaded phone call. At one point, a whole-body tremble swept her. He couldn't hear what the sister was saying but he guessed it was the graphic details of the incident which took her best friend from her forever. He squeezed her hand, reminding her she wasn't alone.

After the call ended, she stared at the floor. No tears. Just a nervous bounce of her knee. He scooted over until their knees touched. Hers stopped shaking.

"Better?" he asked.

"It's never going to be better." She faced him, her eyes clouded in pain. "Life without him." She said it like he needed clarification, but Trevor had experienced the dull ache of loss with heart-wrenching hurt that deadens the soul. When his wife took her last breath, he wished it was him. He didn't envision a future without her in it, but Emma helped absorb the pain as did his re-enlistment and deployment. He gently guided Kacie's head to rest against his shoulder. He'd gotten past that dark season and he'd personally ensure Kacie made it past this.

"His memory will stay alive in your head and your love for him in here." He pointed to his heart. "Believe it or not, things will get better. Davis will be cheering you on from a new place."

"Very profound, Mr. Marlowe. And thoughtful," she mumbled. "And here I thought you were a sexy, single-minded player."

"What?" He shifted his shoulder, forcing her to lift her head. He wanted to view her face. Pain still dulled her eyes but her lips had curled into a smile. He touched her mouth with his index finger. "I like seeing this."

"I like having you here. It helps as does having this assignment away from Colorado and daily reminders of Davy."

"After the way you handled yourself today, I'd say you have a lot of job security."

"Good to know." She stood, folding her arms. "The funeral is in two days. I'll make the reservations today."

"I contacted a mate who has a private plane and he's willing to fly us out tomorrow. He wants to ski in Aspen while we attend the funeral, so he jumped at the chance to have business pay for pleasure." He thrust himself off the bed. "Besides, Freya likes flying private."

"I'll need his information to run a security check." She raised her palm before he could object. "Let me do my job."

The pilot served with him in the SAS and was totally trustworthy, but he acquiesced. She needed purpose.

"I'll forward his info and leave you to sort it." All she'd get would be a vanilla file. The rest would be highly redacted. He stepped toward the door and turned. "We'll all gather tonight in my office for dinner and debrief today as well as strategize."

"I'll be down after I handle this background check." She smiled. "And, Trevor, thanks again for holding my hand today."

"Everyone needs someone to hold onto through the dark times. Glad to be the guy." He paused. "Anything else?"

"We'll need a hotel room. I subleased my apartment to another female employee of Valor."

"Got it." He nodded and smiled, hopeful he'd heard her correctly say a hotel, as in single room. Hell, if he'd clarify. "I'll have Hazel make the reservation."

"See you downstairs."

Trevor wanted to ask her, "What about later? A night cap maybe? In my room?" but instead he muttered a joke about ending the meeting early so she could get her beauty sleep. *I'm such a dork.*

"Oh, take a good look, Mr. Marlowe." She laughed and threw her pillow at his back. "I'm kinda hot."

"You're so right, Miss O'Shea." He closed the door and headed down the hall. *That's why I'll be up all-night lying in bed thinking about you, naked.*

****

Security was a breeze when you fly private. It turned out that Dan, the pilot, was a highly decorated British officer with a heavily redacted file and quite a flirt. She started to believe all these Special Forces guys were irresistible studs.

Had Trevor briefed him on the purpose of their trip, or did the pilot read the room well? The flight out was quiet and uneventful. She rode in one of the two seats in the back and stared out the window most of the way while Trevor and Dan maintained casual conversation in the front via their headphones. Freya slept at her feet, close enough to Trevor to keep an eye on him but her furry comfort as well.

The Rocky Mountains, magnificent year-round, were spectacular in late fall with snow-covered peaks that flowed down their massive sides into valleys where hopeful skiers stood in line for the lifts and their first run of the season down the trails.

The wheels of the plane bounced on the tarmac. Tomorrow would be a sad day. Funerals were never fun. This one might break her. An arm wrapped around her shoulder. A fresh, woody fragrance with a slightly spicy edge pervaded her space. Trevor leaned in and whispered in her ear, "I'll take that." Trevor nodded toward her overnight bag.

"Thanks." She was a Marine and didn't need a man to physically carry her suitcase, but she found it endearing when he came up with a way to lighten her load whether or not that was his intention.

"See you two tomorrow night." Dan gave her a light hug and shook Trevor's hand.

****

Trevor kept his hand in the small of Kacie's back while standing and then held her hand while sitting during the ceremony. The Baptist Church Davy's family chose for the service was small and packed with friends, mostly former military who wanted to pay their respects. He was taken by surprise when Davy's sister asked Kacie to step to the podium and say a few words about Davy. He witnessed her composure as she spoke eloquent words about a man she deeply admired. She took the high road, recounting several funny episodes of Davy bailing her out of trouble while overseas. She ended with a rousing Semper Fi.

On the ride back to the airport, Kacie's mood lifted and she shared some of the good times with Davy. He didn't need to ask if she was okay. He believed she'd experienced closure, and while she would never leave his memory behind, she could concentrate on the positive. Trevor closed the space between them. She curled up in his arms and sighed.

"You want anything before we head home?" Trevor asked as they approached the airport.

"I have everything I need right here." She gazed up at him with a contented half smile.

"We have time if you want to go by the office?"

"Nope. I talked to Vince at the funeral." She tapped her palm on her knee in rhythm to the alternative song playing on the radio. "He's been great allowing me the space I needed to handle this. I'm grateful to have such a sane boss."

"Glad you're in such a good place. Watch out for Dan flying home. He took it easy on you coming here but he's a real stud."

"He is a bit of eye candy." She winked.

When they boarded, Dan ushered Trevor along with Freya to the back and seated Kacie in front next to him. He didn't waste any time putting the moves on Kacie.

Halfway through the flight, Trevor was drooling more than Freya, attempting to keep his cool and be included in the conversation from which Dan cleverly excluded him. The line got crossed when Dan offered to take Kacie on a starlight flight to see the Aurora Borealis.

"Hey, Kacie, trade seats with me. I want to share some news with Dan," Trevor said.

"No problem. I'll spend some quality time with Freya."

Trevor slid into the front seat, fastened his seat belt and put on his headphones.

"What news, mate?" Dan asked.

"Kacie does *not* need to see your cockpit," he said.

Chapter Twelve

One Month Later

Kacie's pulse skyrocketed as Trevor kissed her with this intensity, gently nipping her upper lip, then tracing delicate circles around her mouth. He tasted like forever, well, more like the hint of Spearmint but kissing him was so natural and never got old. She wanted this flutter in her heart forever. Was that even possible? Should she dare to hope?

No new threats or evidence of being watched had presented themselves in the last month. Joe and Sam were given a holiday, which left her to monitor security. She'd offered Hazel tips to determine if she was being followed or watched while shopping. The answer came back, "Negative."

Trevor's eye doctor had cleared him to drive, which also meant he could shoot a gun with his usual proficiency. He still used a cane, but his arm was healing nicely and Freya acted like a third leg.

If she was going to leave, before the holidays would be best. A calendar marking the days as they passed proved Emma's excitement for Christmas. The red-headed munchkin had already compiled a gift list and sworn Kacie to secrecy about one item. She wanted a best friend bracelet from her and confided she'd already made one for Kacie. The kid had grown on her and she'd lost all objectivity on simply being her bodyguard. This was a line she swore she'd never cross. How many lines got crossed before she found herself inept and useless. Aware she was drifting on borrowed time, the talk with Trevor about her returning home was overdue.

"Hey, Trev. When are the guys due back from Thailand?"

"Next week, why?" His brow furrowed.

She checked her surroundings. Hazel was at the grocery store and Emma was upstairs asleep. All she had left was the truth.

"I think it's time for me to return to Valor. My work here appears complete." She pretended to be okay but deep inside she hurt like hell.

"Bloody hell, Kacie." He scowled and hit his cane against the nearby chair. "Way to pull the rug out from under me."

"This must be costing you a fortune, and the reason for hiring me has disappeared." She expected a negative reaction but the intensity of his anger took her by surprise. With her hands rested on her gun belt, she attempted to maintain her cool or appear that way.

"I never figured you for someone who'd run from a fight."

The deep blue of his eyes intensified and bore a hole in her shuttered space. This was a side of Trevor she hadn't experienced before. The lethal side that determines who wins on the battlefield. The key factor in who comes home alive and who arrives in a flag-draped casket.

"How is this a fight?"

"Okay, a challenge." He rolled his eyes. "I met Vince overseas and I can tell you as a Special Forces operator, he lived outside the box of military regulations. The fact we are sharing the same bed won't cause him to blink."

Kacie intimidated most men. Once she outshot them at the gun range and invited them to observe her teach Karate, they ghosted her, but she remained resolute not to lessen her abilities for a sake of a shallow relationship with a beta male. She preferred a man like Trevor who dripped with alpha self-confidence and aggression. He never lorded his skills as a trained sniper or hand-to-hand expert over her but treated her as an equal.

"This isn't easy for me, Trevor. You know I have feelings for you but Valor is understaffed. Vince is requesting more and more frequent updates and an ETA for when I'm headed home."

"I want to come with you and face Vince together." He took a step toward her, a hopeful expression on his face. "I'm partly responsible for your breech in contract."

"I appreciate the offer, Trev, but I don't need anyone fighting my battles for me. Having you there makes me appear weak and Vince won't respect me."

"I see you're determined to leave. Answer one question and be honest."

"Always." She braced herself and wondered if he was going to ask her if she loved him. Was the sex so titillating it masked the real ache and longing that extended into the realm of true love? She'd rather be in his space than anyone else's since she lost Davy. When they shared conversations that explored ideas about esoteric subjects, he captivated her with his insight and intellect. True, the talks usually ended up igniting passion, but not sex. Desire had many faces.

"Was this whole thing," he waved his arms in a large circle, "just a get over?"

****

"What the fuck, Trevor?" Stunned into anger, Kacie charged him, fists bunched. Tears she didn't want flowed down her face.

Unprepared for the assault, he instinctively threw up his arms and blocked her punch but dropped his cane. She stooped to retrieve it.

"Leave it," he yelled, hopping away on his good leg. Freya tucked her tail, dropped her head and followed her master out of the room.

The door slammed and Kacie was alone. The most alone she'd ever been in her life. She gazed out the window at the light sprinkle of snow covering the gardens that had bloomed with a variety of foliage when she arrived but now lay empty. A shiver coursed down her body. Her life resembled that garden, a winter garden where anything living was forced into hibernation. *I wish I could make having to leave okay with Trevor, but I don't think I can.*

Once in her room, she packed her belongings in her duffle bag, then sat on the edge of the bed. How could she leave when Joe and Sam were still absent? If anything happened, she'd never forgive herself.

A light tap-tap at the door sent her hopes soaring, wishing Trevor was on the other end of that knock, calmed and ready to talk. She drew in a deep breath and checked her nerves.

"Come in." She hoped her tone conveyed warm and friendly.

"Hi, Kacie, did Daddy tell you about the Christmas

show?" The little redhead sashayed into the room, obviously spared from the adults acting like children.

"No, little one. What show?" She patted the mattress, indicating for Emma to sit beside her.

"He bought tickets for the three of us, but I think I ruined the surprise." She jutted out her bottom lip. "Please don't tell him."

"Don't worry." Kacie's fingers imitated zipping her lips. "Your secret's safe with me."

"Why is your duffel bag packed?" Emma peered into the unzipped top. "Where are you going?"

Emma's visit caught Kacie by surprise. Her plan had been to develop a story with Trevor to lessen the impact. She guessed it would infuriate Trevor if she excluded him from the conversation, but Emma's wide-eyed expression and longing gaze demanded immediate reassurance.

"A short trip home to check in with the boss." She crossed her fingers behind her back. After all, if she got fired, it could well be a short visit home before she returned to San Diego.

"I thought Daddy was your boss?"

"Well, he kind of is but temporary." She tugged one of Emma's pigtails.

"I don't want you to go, even for a little bit." Her voice squeaked.

The churn in Kacie's stomach which started mid-knock-down-drag-out fight with Trevor intensified into full-blown nausea.

"Be right back, munchkin." She bolted for the bathroom. Once inside, she pressed her body against the closed door and slid to the floor. With deep breaths inhaled in and out, she collected her thoughts and steadied her nerves. The sick feeling in her stomach dissipated, but the corner she had backed herself into still shrunk.

"Hi, Daddy. Kacie's in the bathroom. I don't want her to leave. Tell her to stay."

"Okay, sweetheart. Do me a favor. Go downstairs and get a bottle of water for me, will you?"

"Sure."

A heavy knock sounded on the door. "I'll be right out." She stood up and splashed water on her face. *I'm ready for round two.*

Chapter Thirteen

Kacie swung open the door with a laser gaze that pierced his inner core.

Trevor took a step back. He did not want this fight to continue. Kacie's chest wasn't rising and falling. Is she holding her breath?

"I've accepted that you're determined to leave. I don't like it but I've accepted it."

Her shoulders relaxed and she inhaled a large breath, then sighed but her concentrated focus remained.

"I need a favor." He held up three fanned tickets. "I bought these thinking you'd be here for Christmas. Emma's idea. It would mean a lot to her." *And me.*

Kacie held up her hand. "I'll do it...for Emma." She brushed past him and left the bedroom.

He stuffed two of the tickets in his shirt pocket and flung the third one on her bed.

"The show's this weekend," he muttered.

"Here, Daddy," Emma said, her hand outstretched with a bottle of water.

"Thanks." He placed his hand on her shoulder. "You're the best. You know that?"

"You're not mad at me for loose lips?"

"Of course not." He laughed. "Where did you hear that phrase 'loose lips'?"

"I heard you telling Kacie that loose lips sink ships.

I asked Hazel what it meant and she said it's when someone has a secret, like you and Kacie, and one of you tells. What's your secret, Daddy?"

"Well, if I told you, it wouldn't be a secret anymore." He quickly diverted the direction of the conversation. "Good news, princess. Kacie is going with us to the Christmas show."

Emma squealed and danced in circles. "How many days? Show me on your fingers."

Trevor held up three fingers. *Three days of palpable tension. Three days for me to come up with a plan to change her mind.*

****

Kacie scanned the garage parking lot at The Keegan Theater for anything or anyone suspicious. There were no paneled vans or motorcycles near where they parked in the handicapped spaces. Motorcycles in these temperatures would have raised a red flag but the area was clear. With her head on a swivel, she signaled Trevor that it was okay to exit.

It had been a rocky few days between them, but after late nights spent discussing the consequences of various options, they'd restored the previous easy rhythm of being under the same roof. There was no sex but the heated glances between them signaled desire and tested her self-restraint. On the one occasion they physically bumped into each other, she froze, consumed by the heat that pulsed in her crotch, matched only by the fast thump in her chest. With Joe and Sam back in the residence next week, she could keep some space between them.

Emma grabbed her hand and tugged her toward the entrance. First on her agenda was locating Santa and sharing her wish list. Per the website, he would be seated in the lobby.

Trevor wasn't privy to the items on that list and Kacie only knew of one gift. Emma used the 'loose lips' phrase again, claiming it was between her and Santa. It had become her favorite catch-all justification.

While the other patrons oohed and awed at the Christmas decorations and exclaimed excitement about the upcoming show, she verified the security of the building was as described on their website. It was decent with metal detectors and only two viable exits. Though she remained alert, the lack of any threats allowed her to ease her constant surveillance mode into the enjoyment of Emma's awe.

Midway through the show, Trevor signaled he and Freya were stepping out for a few minutes. Kacie grabbed for his arm to stop him but he quickly hobbled up the aisle. She'd have a word with him later about breaking the rules. There was no possible way to protect him if he was out of her sight. *Damn.* A few minutes later, Emma whispered she needed to go to the bathroom. Her seat wiggle indicated waiting for Trevor to return wasn't an option.

Emma insisted she was a big girl and could handle the bathroom by herself. Kacie waved her into the room and stood by the only exit after moving a cleaning-in-progress sign in the middle of the entrance. Her phone beeped with a text from Trevor.

—*Downstairs bribing Santa*—Trevor added a smiley face.

Flunk for breaking security protocols. — She typed furiously. —*We're at the ladies' bathrooms. Get your ass up here*— She glanced up at the number of women stacked up outside the bathroom awaiting their turn. —*I don't like this. It must be intermission. Too many people.*

—*Give me a few minutes.* —

—*Hurry. Crowd growing up here.* — Kacie scowled at the screen, emotionally charged beyond her normal rational reaction.

"Emma, honey, done yet?" Kacie couldn't see Emma but called into the bathroom space, now crowded with women who ignored the cleaning-in-progress sign.

—*Got wish list Emma gave Santa.* — Trevor added a 100% emoji.

"Emma?" Kacie called louder this time, ignoring Trevor's text. No answer. Her gut tightened as she dashed to the stall Emma had entered. "Emma?" She squatted to peer under the bottom of the door and glimpsed a woman's red, high heels. Panic spiked her adrenaline and she slammed her fist into the door. She checked each stall in a stooped walk before exiting the area.

"Has anyone seen a small redheaded girl wearing a green velvet dress?" Kacie asked as she moved past the line of women waiting in the hall.

"Yes." One of the women stepped forward. "I saw her talking to an olive-skinned woman a minute ago," she said.

"Where did they go?" Kacie grabbed the woman's shoulders.

The woman clutched her purse to her chest with one hand, clearly surprised by Kacie's aggression and pointed toward the exit sign at the end of the hall.

Kacie sprinted the short distance through the

narrow corridor to the metal door with a red exit sign and yanked it open. She leaned over the railing and didn't see anyone, but an accented female voice sternly said, "Hurry," and sounded like it was one flight down. No way she'd let them reach the external door. In a daring move, Kacie vaulted over the rail to the landing below, smashed into the woman and knocked her against the wall. Stunned, the kidnapper cursed Kacie as she regained her balance and withdrew a long-bladed knife. Kacie secured Emma behind her as the much heavier female charged. A wide swipe at Kacie's throat offered the Marine the perfect opportunity to disarm her attacker. The knife clanged to the floor. In seconds, Kacie had the perpetrator face down on the concrete floor, her knee in the woman's back. She used a long silk scarf to hog tie her, aware it was considered excessive force by law enforcement. No way this bad actor would escape. There was hell to pay.

Emma hugged Kacie, muttering between sniffles while glancing between the knife and the captive. Kacie stooped on one knee, inspecting the blotchy little face and runny nose. She tucked an errant red strand of hair behind the girl's ear.

"You're safe, Emma," she said, folding the child into her arms.

"I'm sorry. I know you and Daddy told me not to talk to strangers, but the lady had candy." Emma broke into a sob. "She said Daddy fell and got hurt and she'd take me to him."

"Why didn't you come find me?" Kacie asked.

"I saw you on the phone and you looked angry." She gazed up at Kacie with tearful eyes as she swiped her hand under her nose.

Kacie's shoulders sagged. The words, wretched and inadequate, hung on her like a yoke. Fatigue swamped her but she continued to cradle Emma. This was her fault. She took her eye off the ball, distracted by Trevor. In her training as a Marine, one of Davy's mottos he swore by was, 'Don't bring shame upon yourself or the Marines.' She failed him. She failed Emma and Trevor. Shame rained down.

Chapter Fourteen

Trevor, frantic with worry when his texts and calls went unanswered, notified venue security that his daughter and her protection agent went missing. He hoped to shortcut the search because of their familiarity with the building. His next call was to Joe, which went to voice mail. His message was brief.

"Danger close. Come armed." He ended with the address of the theater.

While the off-duty policeman directed his subordinates to cordon off the exits, he retrieved the wish list Emma gave Santa and held it under Freya's nose. The dog, upon receiving the command to seek, raced up the stairs to the auditorium and sniffed outside the closed doors. Kacie's last text relayed they were in the lady's restroom. Trevor scanned the area, located the bathroom, and commanded Freya down the hall. After a quick run-through of the bathroom, the dog ran to the exit door and barked like her life depended on it. She lunged at the door with bounced glances back at him. Excess saliva drooled from her mouth.

I'm coming Emma. He opened the door and caught his breath when he saw the number of stairs to navigate with his bum leg. Freya was a service dog and not a military canine trained to take down an enemy combatant, but she possessed all the protective instincts of a German Shepherd. He signaled her to seek.

Trevor cursed each step as he descended the flight of stairs, opting to hold onto the rail and hop rather than be slowed by using his cane. Voices combined with yips echoed up the stairwell as he rounded the corner to the first floor.

The scene was chaotic but he viewed it with relief. Freya eyed him first and barked, sending all eyes in his direction. He focused on Emma, who sprung from Kacie's embrace and ran to him.

"Daddy. Kacie saved me from the bad lady." She pointed to the female body being helped to a standing position by the off-duty cop.

"Glad you're safe, sweet girl." He kissed the top of her head before lifting her into his arms, using the wall to steady his stance. Aware Kacie's gaze was fixed on him, he ignored her, angry she'd let the kidnapping attempt get this far. Instead, he nodded to the policeman.

"Where are you taking her?"

"I'm locking her in my office until the on-duty patrol shows up. I assume you want to press charges?"

"I'd like to question her first. Is there a private place I can use?"

"Want me to be there?" Kacie asked.

"No," he said, maintaining a steady gaze on the woman. "Joe and Sam are on their way to escort you and Emma home." Out of the corner of his eye, he glimpsed her open her mouth and held up his hand at full stop. "I need you to get Emma safely home. You think you can do that?"

He whipped his head around and sent her a look he reserved for an enemy combatant right before he pulled the trigger to send them to Paradise. He set Emma down and withdrew his wallet from his back pocket and flipped it open, revealing his identification and credentials to the officer. He noticed recognition from the officer.

"Were you in the military?" the cop asked, as if to verify Trevor's identity.

"Yes, British SAS," Trevor said, "but you knew that," and flipped the wallet closed. "Could we keep the media out of this? I suspect the trail from this incident will lead to a terrorist plot that exceeds local jurisdiction."

"Depends on whether she's here legally and whether you press charges. If you do, eventually there will be a trial and public exposure."

"I searched her and found a fake driver's license. I believe she's here illegally and can be deported. No fuss, no muss, no media," Kacie said. "I also found out where she was supposed to take Emma." She stared at Trevor. "I wasn't here twiddling my thumbs before you arrived on the scene." She puffed a heavy breath.

"If she doesn't show up soon, her associates will scatter like roaches." Trevor checked his watch. "Where?"

The other two security guys opened the back door to the outside, and entered, accompanied by Joe and Sam who had guns drawn.

"Easy boys," Trevor said, nodding toward Emma.

"Daddy, I want to go home." Emma tugged at his sleeve.

"Okay, sweetheart. Kacie and Joe will take you and I'll be home soon with Sam."

"Lock it down." He signaled for Joe and Kacie to leave.

"Entrance of Rock Creek Parkway," Kacie whispered as she passed him.

"Thanks." His anger lessened with the realization she'd gathered vital intel in a short amount of time. He squeezed her arm.

"Happy hunting," she said, withdrawing from his grip.

****

Angry that Trevor blamed her for the attempted kidnapping, Kacie rode in sullen silence back to the house. Joe engaged Emma with small talk, which worked to distract her from the recent danger. Thankful he didn't ask her any questions, Kacie stared out the window, mentally sapped and emotionally drained. Joe discreetly checked his rearview and his side mirror for any unwelcomed tails. She could tell from his easy demeanor nothing concerned him.

She texted Vince she'd be heading back to Winding Creek in the next day or two and requested he speak to Trevor about a suitable replacement. She understood her communication would open a Pandora's box of consequences. So be it.

Hazel met them at the front porch but seemed uninformed about the close call. Joe could brief her while Kacie got Emma settled in. She and Joe would conduct a thorough review of security later. She didn't want to be accused a second time of a security lapse.

Hazel approached her while she warmed herself in front of the fire, a concerned expression on her face, and holding a tray with a cup of hot tea and a plate of cookies. Kacie had grown close to the family, and Hazel was no exception. A woman of empathy and compassion, Kacie counted on her as a counterweight to Trevor's intensity.

"Have a seat, dear," Hazel said. She laid the tray on the coffee table and sat in the chair closest to the sofa.

Kacie obeyed like a ten-year-old schoolgirl. She peered at the array on the fine China plate.

"Have a biscuit," she said with a smile, "or two."

"Thank you, Hazel." She selected a chocolate wafer and nibbled the end.

"Joe told me what happened." She patted Kacie's hand. "This isn't your fault, my dear."

Kacie poured a few drops of honey into the hot tea and stirred. Her gaze fixated on the arrangement of colorful glass balls in the center of the table. A mental image of Trevor's stone-cold expression as he rounded on her bore into her mind. She couldn't unsee the warm cobalt blue eyes turning icy. She couldn't numb the sting of rejection.

"I think I've fallen in love with him, Hazel." She sipped the hot drink.

"And he with you, my dear."

"I doubt that. If you could have seen the hate in his eyes…." Kacie swiped at a tear as it rolled down her cheek.

"I doubt it was hate. I've known Trevor since he was a young lad. Fear maybe masked as hate. I witnessed the look you're describing when he got the news his wife was terminal. I thought he might go gunning for the doctor who gave him the news."

"Thanks for the reassurance but it's too late."

"It's never too late."

"Where's Emma?" She swung her head around. "I don't want her to see me upset."

"She's asleep upstairs. All the excitement tired her

out."

"Excitement is a nice way of putting what happened." Kacie used her palm to wipe an escaped tear that hung on her chin.

"If I hadn't been so preoccupied by Trevor texting me, I would have seen the tango luring Emma away. He's a total distraction anytime I'm around him. I lose awareness of my surroundings, which in my line of work is unacceptable."

"Trevor has responsibility for this as well. I'll see to it he realizes his share of the blame."

Kacie gulped her last sip of tea and placed the cup back on the tray. She's arranged with Joe to take the third shift. Hopefully Trevor would be home and asleep while she held watch.

"Thanks for everything, Hazel. I've requested my agency contact Trevor about a replacement." *God knows what he'll say about me. I might be driving home to a pink notice.*

"Get some sleep, Kacie. I'll leave your dinner in the refrigerator." She smiled warmly and exited with the tray.

Kacie's gaze flicked around the room. A chill skidded down her body. She moved in front of the fireplace for warmth and rubbed her arms, but the chill had penetrated her heart.

Chapter Fifteen

Neither had said the "L" word but the desire, the longing, and the simple brightening of his spirit when she entered the room spoke volumes about his feelings for Kacie. Why had he been such an asshole at the theater? She tried to hide the hurt at his dismissal, but when her chin trembled, he ignored her. If he was honest with himself, expecting her to engage in a relationship with him while enduring the hardship of her mission, her recent loss of Davy, all of it, was selfish.

Kacie had extracted excellent intel from the would-be kidnapper, in the U.S. illegally from Mali, leaving him and Sam free to pursue the person who hired her. The guy in charge of the attack was in the exact named location but when approached by the police, opened fire and was killed. His credentials were also fake. Neither one of them were on the terror watch list. He suspected they were low-level expendables. With the exception they'd learned both the bad actors were African, they were back to square one with leads.

It was close to three a.m. when he and Sam arrived back home. Freya wagged her tail and whimpered as Trevor unlocked the front door. Sam entered first and was greeted by Joe.

"Any problems?" Trevor asked.

"Nope. Condition Yellow for the residence and its

occupants." He patted Freya's head. "What happened on your end?"

"The intel Kacie gathered checked out, but the dude didn't want to talk to us." He rolled his eyes. "The cop who accompanied us dropped him when he opened fire."

"Shit. That's tough luck. What about the woman?"

"We got what we could from her, which wasn't much, but she's no longer a threat."

"Dead?" Joe asked.

"No. Not yet."

"Meaning?" Joe rubbed his chin.

"We shipped her back to Mali with trackers implanted in her clothes and one injected in the fat tissue of her hip, under the guise of treating her injury from Kacie tackling her. We hope she'll run straight to the real bosses."

"Do we have active tactical units in that region of Africa?"

"We do and they're a specialized Marine unit. Total bad asses." Trevor smiled. "This nightmare's coming to an end soon, bro."

"Time to feed my girl." Trevor said. "You hungry, Freya?" He slapped the side of his leg and moved toward the kitchen door.

"Speaking of 'your girl'...." Joe pointed to the kitchen, his eyes so wide, it furrowed his brow.

Trevor hesitated at the door, staring at the blue colored wooden frame. Was she waiting for him with a broom handle or maybe an iron skillet? He glanced at Freya, then at Joe. With a roll of his shoulders, he pushed open the swinging door. Freya dashed in, her head bowed and her tail wagging. Kacie stood at the kitchen sink, a glass of water in her hand. Freya pawed her leg, obviously anxious for her attention. He was also anxious for her attention and a heart-to-heart conversation with an apology for being an asshole.

"How's it going?" he asked in a barely audible voice.

Kacie didn't look up from her crouched position petting Freya. "I'll get her some food." She stood and moved to the cabinet, maintaining diverted attention from him as she methodically prepared the mixture of canned and dry food. "She must be hungry."

Loneliness wrapped around him in a tight seal. He'd rather be screamed at or pounded on but not ignored. In a desperate attempt to connect on any level with her, he stepped forward and gripped her arm. She responded by grabbing the glass of water and tossing it in his face.

"It's going something like that, Trevor," she said with her body braced, and her hands fisted by her sides.

Surprised by her response, he sputtered and wiped the water out of his eyes.

"Better than a frying pan or a broom handle," he said with a laugh and an attempt at levity.

"I think water was the appropriate symbol."

"Symbol of how mad you are at me?" He reached for a nearby kitchen towel.

"No, symbol of us being washed up." She shoved him and tried to pass but he blocked her exit.

He wrapped his muscular arms around her chest and held her, resting his head on her shoulder. The familiar lavender scent flooded him with memories. He breathed in the smell and held his breath, as if trying to preserve the celebration of pleasure.

A sharp pain snapped him into the present and commanded his attention. Kacie's elbow connected with his stomach with enough force for him to release his hold.

"Fuck, that hurt."

"So did embarrassing and belittling me."

"I'm sorry. I know I hurt you."

"You blamed me for the breech in security when you, in a completely cavalier manner, ignored all the rules of not getting separated in public." She stomped her foot. "Your arrogant disregard for safety almost got Emma kidnapped."

"I texted and called you, but you didn't answer."

"I was a little busy. If we'd been together then all the back and forth wouldn't have been necessary and I wouldn't have been distracted."

"I thought we were code yellow and the threat level was low." He hung his head. "I wanted to do something special for Emma. She's been so sequestered for the past months and hasn't complained once about it."

"Rules are rules, Trevor. We have security protocol for a reason. You know that."

He did know and in a stark moment of epiphany, all the toughness and alpha bravado crumbled. He almost lost his daughter.

"I'm who they want. Why don't those fuckers come after me and take their best shot?" he said, catching his breath between words. "Emma's a six-year-old child. She's innocent and doesn't deserve this. I brought trouble home with me." His chest heaved in short bursts between words.

"That's exactly what they're doing, Trevor. The point of terrorists is to create holy terror in their target.

You." She laid her hands on his chest. "You'll nail these mother fuckers."

Kacie was the strongest woman he'd ever met. Accustomed to being the one in control of men who rarely questioned his choices, she could hold her own. In this case, she was correct to dress him down.

"Kacie, I don't want to fight." He exhaled a heavy sigh. "I hired you to protect us and violated your trust by ignoring the procedures you put in place. It won't happen again." He clasped her hands in his.

"I accept your apology." She pulled her hands from his grasp. "Emma's safe and that's what matters."

"You matter to me." He tugged her close. "I want to kiss you but I'm afraid you'll hurt me." He grunted as he rubbed his stomach.

With her eyes half-closed, she parted her lips. "Truce," she whispered.

Trevor moaned as his lips touched hers, softly at first, then with a fevered need, he clutched her bottom and pulled her into him, kissing her face and her neck like it was his last chance.

****

Kacie leaned into the kiss. She rationalized it was okay because this moment needed to last. It was probably the last time she'd see Trevor. She hadn't revealed her plan to leave but it was only a matter of time before Vince reached out to him about the replacement. He tugged her closer to his body. His erection pressed hard on her stomach and titillated her desire. She wrapped her leg around his thigh and ground into his crotch. He slid one arm under her raised leg and lifted her, and while cradling her ass in his other arm, hobbled backward to the kitchen table, reclining her face up on the oak planks. Trevor wasted no time stripping off his shirt and kicking off his pants. She viewed his well-muscled chest with the V-shaped pattern of hair collapsing into a happy trail. The ache between her legs canceled any concern one of the guys or God help her, Hazel or Emma could walk in right now.

While she traced the outline of his nipples with her index finger, he unfastened her bra strap and let it fall from her breasts. Kacie lifted her t-shirt over her head and tossed it to the floor along with her bra. Before she could resume fondling his nipples, he snagged one of hers between his teeth. At the same time grabbing the other one and gently rotating it between his thumb and finger. She closed her eyes and moaned as her head fell back.

"I want you," she said in a guttural tone.

"Not yet," he whispered, sliding her to the edge of the table and bending her knees.

"I can't last," she said as he spread her legs and bowed his head between them.

The warmth spread both into her stomach and down her legs. Her body tightened as it prepared for release. She uttered a continuous grunting moan as the throbbing built into an explosion of intense pleasure.

"That's it, baby," he said, easing himself into her.

The heat from his body as he entered her combined with the tingling of her own release made it difficult to match his thrust, so she wrapped her arms around his neck and let him take her.

"Spend the rest of the night with me?" Trevor asked, handing her the clothes she hadn't been able to take off fast enough.

"I don't think staying here is a good idea," she said, unable to look him in the eye.

"Are you still miffed at me?" He tossed his shirt over his head, then brushed his fingers through his hair.

"Not as long as you admit you were wrong?" She chuckled.

"I agree I broke security. It won't happen again." Trevor pulled up his pants, zipped and buttoned them. "I want to lay this entire FUBAR to rest. Are we good?"

She couldn't honestly say they were good with the same meaning Trevor implied but she didn't harbor any anger. In fact, today's events served as a lesson. It's one thing to read a list of rules and sign off that you'll follow them. It's quite another to experience the effects of breaking them. Realism got real today as Davy used to say.

"Trevor, we need to talk."

"I know what you're going to say. Save it. Get some shut eye. We'll hash it out tomorrow." He patted his leg for Freya to follow and exited through the kitchen door.

This won't end well, no matter what I do. My bags are packed. It'd be easier on everyone if I slipped, no, slithered out tonight and headed for Colorado.

She ascended the stairs two at a time with the sole purpose of grabbing her duffle bag and slipping out the back door. By the time her car engine alerted the guys, she'd be halfway down the street to the beltway exit.

The bag was under the bed where she left it. She grabbed her toothbrush and toothpaste and dropped them in a side pocket. With one last look around the room, she heaved the bag over her shoulder, and with the stealth of a feral cat, crept back down the stairs.

The path through the living room to the back door was unlit and little ambient light shone through the heavy curtains. She had memorized the furniture placement as part of her indoor security, but as she picked her way through the room, she hit something hard. The object, most likely a chair, belonged in the corner but was out of place in the middle of the open space.

The bright beam of a flashlight shone in her face and blinded her. She dropped the bag and rolled, coming upright in a fighting stance.

"You going somewhere?"

"Sam! What the fuck?" She blew out a breath and relaxed her posture.

"What the fuck indeed, Kacie."

Chapter Sixteen

Kacie stepped to Sam and redirected the tactical flashlight aimed at her face.

"It's best if I leave, Sam."

"Best for who?" He turned on a low beam lamp and pressed the off button of the flashlight.

She flopped down on the chair she'd just stumbled over and leaned forward with her elbows on her knees. The last thing she wanted was to drag Sam into the fray.

"Best for everyone. I've clearly lost my focus and—"

"Whoa, whoa, whoa." Sam's voice rose with each utterance. "You're one of the finest operators I've ever worked with." He hesitated. "And I'll add, the hottest although I know I don't stand a chance with Trevor laying claim."

"First of all, no one 'claims' me." *Sam knows?* "You know Trevor and I…are involved?"

"Of course I know. I'm a trained observer and I'm good at my job."

"Thanks for the compliment and despite the fact I shot you?" She suppressed a grin.

"You winged me." He brushed his leg. "Trevor gave us orders to stand down but we were acting like cowboys. What happened is on us."

"Copy that." She eyed her duffle bag. "I hate goodbyes, especially when the decision to leave hurts like hell. I can't begin to know what to say to Emma. I wasn't supposed to get attached." She interlaced her hands on top of her head. "I've really made a mess of things."

"I'll tell you straight. Exiting like this is some chicken shit move and not who you are. Take your duffle bag upstairs and get some shut-eye. You secret is safe with me."

"Thanks, Sam." She thumped her heart with her fist. "I do have one favor." She reached into her duffle bag and pulled out a small, wrapped box with a glitter-covered red bow. "I bought this for Emma for Christmas. Would you put it someplace where she'll find it if I'm not here?"

"Sure, but I hope you can give the gift to her yourself." Sam tucked the box into his jacket. "Christmas is less than a week away."

The wood step near the bottom of the staircase creaked, a noise both Sam and Kacie familiarized themselves with as part of their security protocol for the house. Sam grabbed the duffel bag and tossed it behind the sofa seconds before the hall light flicked on.

Trevor, known as 'The Iceman' by his Special Forces team, personified the moniker at this moment. With his hair tousled and his unshaven cheeks and chin, he appeared rougher than usual, like don't want to meet you in a dark alley, rougher.

"What did I miss?" He glanced between them with his gaze lingering on Kacie.

"I'm on watch until six a.m. sir," Sam said.

Kacie fidgeted with her bangs but stayed silent. *Could I be any more uncomfortable?*

"Couldn't sleep?" Trevor directed his attention to

Kacie.

"No, as a matter of fact."

"Me either," he said and ran his hand through his hair. "Care to join me for chamomile tea?" He waved his hand toward the kitchen.

She nodded in reply but wondered if he could see the rapid thud of her aching heart pounding against her chest. The moment of truth had arrived. Sam was right. Fleeing in the middle of the night wasn't her style. Her knees shook but she thrust herself off the cushion and followed him into the kitchen. A shiver trembled through her body. What if she called Vince, told him she'd broken her contract, slept with her client and almost got his daughter kidnapped? What if she totally blew up her life? She'd never work in the private security business again but with one well-aimed blow, her internal turmoil would end and she could live happily ever after with the man she'd been waiting for most of her adult life.

His shirtless back was to her, busy fixing the tea. Despite the fact he hadn't been able to work out as hard as usual, every defined muscle rippled as he moved. The scar on his arm was permanent and sexy, better than any tattoo. She waited for him to turn toward her.

"I owe you the truth." She concentrated on keeping her hand steady as he handed her the cup of hot tea.

"I know the truth, Kacie. I know you love me."

"True and in a perfect world—"

"It's never going to be perfect. The world is messed up and we both understand the evil that exists, but together we can create our own four walls. It'll be what we make it, which could be damn fine."

"I'm compelled to go back and face Vince and

make this right. Otherwise, I'll live with a black cloud over my head. I'm still a Marine and not taking responsibility would be to dishonor my brothers and sisters."

"Your mind is made up?"

"Yes. I called Vince about ending my tour and finding you a suitable replacement."

"You're breaking my heart, Kacie." He set his cup on the table with enough force to cause a spill. "Was that your duffle bag Sam tossed over the sofa?"

"You saw that, huh?" She tried for levity, but his somber expression remained. "Yes. I was going to leave tonight so I didn't inflict anymore pain, but he talked me out of it."

"Too late." He stood and returned his cup to the counter. "I'll call Vince tomorrow morning."

"I'll stay until the replacement gets here and help groove her in."

"No need." He kept his back to her as he approached the kitchen door. "He can probably have someone here tomorrow night. Get some sleep. You have a hell of a drive."

Chapter Seventeen

Kacie drove straight through to the outskirts of Denver without spending the night. A few cat naps in truck stops and copious amounts of black coffee and junk food fueled her trip. Driving was an art, one she thrived on perfecting, although she preferred sharp turns and windy roads to the steady pace of the interstate. Still, the quiet of the open road late at night offered her solace and perspective she didn't find elsewhere.

Exhausted but relieved to be home, she checked into a hotel. She'd sublet her apartment in Winding Creek and didn't feel like answering questions to the agency newbie who'd leased it. After she caught up on her sleep, she'd meet with Vince and find out if she still had a job, still had a career using the only employment skills she possessed.

Sam texted her and inquired if she had arrived home safely. He added the house had a strange emptiness with her gone, and joked the only one bossing him around in her absence was Hazel. He also mentioned the new female bodyguard was 'fugly' as hell. She texted back it served him right for being such a playboy, emphasis on boy and confirmed her trip home was tiring but uneventful. At least he still spoke to her but no mention of Trevor and she refused to ask.

The rumble of snowplows woke Kacie. She rolled

out of bed and peered out the window at the dense white flakes cascading to an already snow-covered landscape. The hotel crew had blowers clearing the sidewalks to the parking lot, where many of the cars sported red bows on their hoods and a few had fake reindeer antlers attached to the windows. *Gotta love the spirit of the West.*

A loud knock on the door startled her. She checked her watch. *Oh, my fricking god, it's ten o'clock. I redefined the meaning of 'slept in' for a Marine.*

A second knock, more like a double tap, sent her scrambling for her jeans and sweatshirt.

"Just a minute," she called out. She tugged the black sweatshirt over her head, *sans* bra, and fastened the button on her jeans.

A familiar voice answered. "Kacie, it's Gil."

"Gilbert O'Shaughnessy," she said as she flung open the door. "I'll be damned."

"Welcome home, Marine." He squinted his eyes as he read aloud the logo imprinted on her shirt. "Front toward Enemy." He hugged her. "That's my girl."

"How did you know I was here?" She waved him into the room and shut the door.

"Here at this hotel or here in Denver?"

"God, Gil, you're such a tool." She laughed. "Either."

"Vince told me. He asked me to fetch you for the company Christmas banquet."

"Christmas banquet?" *I thought I heard you say, firing squad.* "Wait, it's Christmas? Today?"

"Man, you really are sleep deprived. It's Christmas Eve." He glanced around the room. "It's the one day a year when we dress up."

"I have a few nice dresses at my apartment in Winding Creek." She turned up her palms. "When is the dinner?"

"Not until five p.m., but the roads are a mess and a new storm is forecast for later today."

"If I leave now, I can make it before they close the exits on I-25." She grabbed her purse and motioned for Gil to come with her.

"I have a four-wheel-drive vehicle." He jangled a set of keys in the air. "Leave your muscle car here. Vince prepaid your room for a few more days until he can find new housing for your renter."

"Nice of him," she said. *The shit might not be as deep as I thought, but I doubt Vince knows about my affair.*

"Grab your bag in case we get stranded. You might be forced to stay at my place in Winding Creek for the night." He waggled his eyebrows.

"You're such a nerd." Kacie punched him in the arm. "It's good to be home, Gil."

****

Freezing rain mixed with snow drizzled down on Kacie and Gil as they arrived at Bolton's Valor Security and Investigations. She clung to Gil as they entered the building using slippery ice as the excuse, but her frayed nerves betrayed her.

"You're among friends, Kacie," Gil said, empathy obvious in his tone.

"Am I that obvious?" she said, adjusting her rhinestone bejeweled shawl.

"You look stunning." His gaze scanned her from head to toe. "All eyes will be locked on you, so pull it together." He smiled. "Or, fake it."

The building, decorated in red and green and gold, signaled Christmas as Vince's favorite holiday. The twelve foot fir tree in the lobby riveled the one she'd seen on the news in Denver's downtown center. Stacks of wrapped presents lay underneath in disarray, as if someone tossed them from a large red sack. *I don't have gifts.*

"Those gifts are all from Vince to the employees. He requested no gifts for himself and instead asked everyone to donate to The Special Forces Foundation." Gil patted her arm. "No worries, Kacie."

"What, are you a mind reader now?" Kacie teased.

The scent of cinnamon and clove and roast beef wafted through the air as they entered the wide hallway, with staff gathered around the catered banquet table. She thought her eyeballs might pop at the dessert table. The party, in full swing, came to an abrupt halt when someone started clapping. Everyone turned in her direction. They clapped in unison…for her. After a couple of wolf whistles rang out, she mouthed thank you to the crowd of co-workers and secretly wished for rescue from all the attention.

Out of the corner of her eye, she caught a glimpse of Vince, a beverage in his hand, making his way toward her.

Gil nodded to Vince. "Told you," he whispered in her ear and melted into the crowd.

"Glad you could make it tonight." He glanced around the room. "We pull out all the stops for Christmas." Vince handed her a glass. "Tequila Sunrise?"

"Thanks." She accepted the glass and took a large gulp, but would have preferred to chug it down.

"Umm." She coughed and cleared her throat. "The bartender didn't hold back on the tequila."

"Enjoy." He chuckled. "We have cots set up for the over-imbibers." He peered out the set of glass windows at the white-out conditions. "Or in case we get snowed in."

"I'm good. Gil is my designated driver, *and* he comes equipped with four-wheel drive."

"Gil is one squared away dude."

"Thanks for comping the hotel room. Much appreciated."

"Least I could do after the stellar job you did for Trevor." He smiled. "Business talk is forbidden today and tomorrow is Christmas, but we'll talk first thing Thursday." He winked.

"Here's to an even more successful next year." He tapped her glass in an informal toast.

Kacie's stomach flipped. *Vince doesn't know.* Guilt seeped into her consciousness. She'd received a hero's welcome from the team. The people believed her to be a person who followed the rules. Her chest tightened, making it difficult to breathe. She turned the glass upside down and chugged.

****

The rich, inviting aroma of coffee wafted under his nostrils. The fragrant, slightly sweet aroma reminded him of Kacie. Who was brewing coffee this early on Christmas Day?

Trevor had fallen asleep in his recliner last night after hours of assembling the pink bicycle with attached training wheels he'd bought for Emma. It was number one on the secret list she gave Santa. Daylight started to creep in through the curtains. He shook off the drowsiness and decided to join whoever was in the kitchen in a cup of coffee.

"Hi, boss," Sam said, pouring himself a cup.

"Pour me one, would you?"

"Late night?" Sam handed him a steaming cup of brew.

"Yeah. I can assemble an M4 Carbine rifle blindfolded, but Emma's bicycle…." He smacked his forehead, then took a seat on the stool at the bar. "Will you and Joe join us for Christmas dinner? Hazel prepared a proper feast." Before Sam could answer, Trevor read the scroll on the mug and burst out laughing. "Cluster Fuck Fixer." He read it aloud.

"Merry Christmas," Sam said. "It comes with a velvet sack for when Emma's around."

"Speaking of…. I hear a familiar squeal in the living room. She's up early. Good thing I downed the cookies left for Santa." He stood, gulped his coffee and handed the mug to Sam.

"I'll check the perimeter," Sam said.

"Dinner is at four, sharp." He turned toward the door.

"Daddy, daddy, look what Kacie got me?" Emma burst through the door holding a small box with a red bow. "Can I open it now, please?"

"Where did that come from?" Trevor's gaze drifted off to the side. "I don't remember seeing it under the tree."

"I found it on my dresser this morning when I woke up. Santa must have delivered it for her."

"Santa is a sneaky bastard." Trevor glared at Sam.

"Daddy, quarter in the cuss jar, right now." She placed her hands on her hips.

Sam reached around to the corner shelf and handed the jar to Trevor with a grin.

"Rain check." He handed the jar back to Sam, who laid it on the shelf and hurried out the side door.

Emma started to yank at the ribbon on top of the box. He thought he'd laid his heart to rest after he filed the final action report to Vince, but as Emma tugged at the bow, the memories of Kacie yanked at his heart.

His report laid out her quick action and heroism in rescuing Emma. He raved about her competence as part of his security detail and although loss torched him as he typed the words, remarked about her complete devotion to upholding the high standards of the Marine Corps.

Emma danced around in glee. A colorful beaded bracelet dangled from her small hand. She twirled in circles, exclaiming she loved it.

He should be happy because the gift brought his little girl joy, but red-hot anger surged up his neck. Kacie should have asked permission but instead he had the feeling she manipulated Sam to perpetrate the location of the gift where Emma would see it first before he had a chance to decide if Kacie should stay in Emma's life.

"Daddy, what does it say?" She held up the bracelet. It had an engraved plate with the word 'Bestie' and a heart.

The hopeful expression on his daughter's face transformed to one of complete contentment when he read the inscription. His anger dissipated. Her happiness was paramount.

"Put it on my wrist, please, Daddy." She curled into the curve of his body.

It was a simple clasp she could manage on her own, but he understood she wanted to share this moment with him. In her mind, Kacie belonged to them both.

****

The last thing Kacie remembered from the Christmas Eve party was making snow angels in the parking lot with Gil and a few other tipsy staffers. When she awoke, it took her a minute to recognize she was in Gil's apartment, in his futon bed to be specific. Her red evening dress hung on the closet door. She gasped, afraid she'd find her naked body and a lot of regret under the flannel sheets. Gil's friendship was important to her and if they'd had a one-night stand, he'd expect the last thing she wanted which was a morph into a romantic relationship. She lifted the covers and peered at her body, clothed in a t-shirt and leggings she'd worn under the casual clothes she'd changed into. The night came back to her through the foggy haze of all those Tequila Sunrises. *Ugh.* She rubbed her face. *I need lots of coffee and aspirin.*

She swung her bare feet over the edge of the mattress and found her socks laid out and dry on top of her boots. Her flannel shirt and pants were folded on top of the chair next to the cluttered desk where Gil worked his magic. Where was the computer whiz?

She buttoned her shirt as she stumbled out to the living room, where Gil greeted her with a cup of hot coffee and two ibuprofens.

"Good man," she said before throwing back the pain killers and taking a long gulp.

"A good time was had by all last night. Especially you." He snorted.

"Uh-oh. What did I do?"

"You snuggled up next to me on the drive home and called me Trevor." He tilted his head and sent her a questioning stare. "What's going on, Kacie?"

I could deny it. I could pretend I have no idea what he's talking about but he's coming to me first. I owe him the truth.

"I wish I could make this okay. I got nothing to say other than Trevor and I got too close while I was on assignment. It's why I returned home." She grabbed his hands and looked him square in the eyes. "I do plan to come clean with Vince."

"I know you'll do the right thing, Kacie." Gil said and squeezed her hands.

"You're a great friend and colleague. Are we okay?"

"We're golden, girlfriend. Your only obligation to me is to do your job one hundred percent." He stood and pulled her to her feet. "And from what I can tell, you did that." He fist-bumped her.

"Let's get going. I heard Vince is handing out year-end bonuses today."

"Mind dropping me at the hotel?" She anticipated his shocked reaction and cut off any argument about why she should go by laying her hand over his mouth. "I'm fine. I promise."

They drove to her hotel on deserted streets, in silent awe of the winter wonderland all around them. She collected her things and lifted the door handle to exit.

"You want me to bring a doggie bag by later? Nothing will be open today unless you like Chinese food."

"As a matter of fact, I'm a big fan of Chinese takeout." Kacie laughed. "But I'm exhausted after the long drive and the party last night." She noticed his face paled and his mouth turned down. "I'll check in with you later and if the roads are cleared, I might even drive over." She closed the car door and waved goodbye, secretly grateful for a quiet room and a long nap.

Her phone dinged with notification of a text. She glanced at the sender. *Sam.* The message said, *Call me.*

Chapter Eighteen

Glad she'd opted to stay at her hotel, Kacie grabbed an apple and water in the lobby and headed for her room. Secured inside, she selected Sam's number on her cell phone and hit call.

"Hi, Hot Stuff," Sam said. "I saw on the news a snowmageddon blanketed Denver. You doing okay?"

"I'm tucked away in my hotel room enjoying the down time."

"Spending Christmas alone? That doesn't sound like fun."

"The company had their celebration yesterday on Christmas Eve."

"So my girl is hung over, right?"

"You're very bright for a juvenile." Kacie snickered. "How's things on your end? How is Emma?"

"Why I'm calling. She loved her bracelet and claimed she'll never take it off. She begged her dad to FaceTime you to say thanks. I think she misses you and wants to see your face."

"I'm glad she liked it." She wanted to hear Trevor's reaction to Emma's gift but didn't ask. "Will Trevor initiate the call?"

"Er, uh, no. He handed that task off to me."

"I see." It bothered her Trevor wouldn't be on the call, but at least he didn't block her from talking to Emma. "Wish him a Merry Christmas for me."

"Will do. Hey, a fifty-pound energizer bunny is in my face, hopping from one foot to the other. I'm switching to video."

"Me too," Kacie said with a giggle. She clutched the phone in an anticipatory grip with a smile stretched across her cheeks.

"Here's Emma," Sam said with flair.

****

Kacie experienced a sense of peace and contentment after her call with Emma, who explained she understood Kacie had to work in a different city and would be gone for a while. *Good job, Trevor.* Emma made Kacie promise to wear her gift every day, which she assured Kacie was in the mail. Emma, in her excitement, let it slip she'd made the beaded friendship bracelet with help from Hazel.

Back to work today with a meeting at 10:00 a.m. with the big boss. She pulled into the parking lot early and listened to music for a few minutes before checking her makeup in the mirror and gathering her notebook, weapon, and purse.

The receptionist called out to her as she passed the front desk. An express package had come for her from Virginia. Kacie read the return address and ripped it open with urgency. A colorful beaded bracelet wrapped in red tissue paper was inside. She fitted it on her wrist and held it up to the light. Some of the beads were translucent and glowed. It fit more like armor than jewelry because of the attached sentiment.

Vince stood and shook her hand as she entered his office.

"I understand you skipped out on us yesterday for sleep." He smiled. "Understood, but first things first."

He handed her an envelope. "Your well-deserved bonus."

"Thanks. but I think I'll have you hold on to that until the end of our meeting."

Vince signaled for her to sit in the chair closest to his desk. She dug deep to maintain composure and contemplated how to begin. The more time she interacted with this group, the more validated she felt about her decision to join and hopefully remain.

"You're not quitting, are you?" Vince asked.

"No," Kacie replied. *But I might get fired.*

"Good, because we are short-handed right now. Operators with your experience are hard to find."

Vince was a guy who liked directness, admired brutal honesty, and preferred facts over opinion. She squared her shoulders and rested her tightly clasped hands in her lap.

"I broke a rule in my contract." She stared directly into Vince's eyes.

"That sucks. Which one?" His eyes narrowed.

"I engaged in an off-limits relationship with my client." Heat flooded her neck and face. Death by one thousand cuts would have been less painful than witnessing her boss, who trusted her, drop his head and close his eyes. He cursed under his breath and rubbed his temples.

"That son of a bitch was a stud overseas when I met him. I thought he was acting out over his wife's death but—"

"I accept responsibility for my actions, sir."

"Are you telling me you weren't seduced by Trevor's dashing British charm?" He cocked his head and lifted an eyebrow. "Are you saying you were the aggressor?"

"No, I'm saying I was a willing participant." She wiped her sweaty palms on her pants. "We just clicked."

"I can read between the lines, Kacie." He stood and paced back and forth behind his desk a few strides before stopping in front of her. "I have these rules for a reason and I expect them to be followed. Got it?"

"Yes, sir." She stood with perfect posture. "I'll clear out my desk." She turned to leave, a hollowness in her chest but a righteousness in her heart she'd done the right thing.

"Hold on, Marine." He touched her arm. "Do you believe in redemption?"

"Absolutely." She scanned his face and noticed a gleam in his eyes. "What did you have in mind?"

"Probation. A chance to get squared away."

"I accept."

"You haven't heard the terms."

"I know the definition of squared away, sir."

"Listen. I respect your actions this morning. You owned up to your mistake. I'm not supposed to allow what you've been through personally to cloud my judgement where the operation of the company is concerned, but I'm aware of how grief can affect your decisions. Davy Crockett was important to you."

"He was family to me." A new sadness draped her senses. "I miss him, sir."

"That's why I'm cutting you a break." He lowered his head, nodded, and grinned. "And I'm shorthanded right now." His smile spread across his face. "The terms are simple. This stays between us. You'll be assigned jobs locally, meaning within the state, for ninety days. We'll reevaluate then." He handed her the envelope. "You earned this. Take it."

"Thank you, sir." She patted the envelope in her palm, then stuffed it in her purse.

No longer walking on a knife's edge, she wanted to skip out of his office singing.

The burden that had weighed so heavily on her mind had been lifted. Second chances rocked.

Chapter Nineteen

Three months later

The company was booming. The need for security seemed ever increasing, as was the request for personal protection. Kacie had been assigned to several uber wealthy clients, all of whom were fat, old, and balding. She figured it was Vince's quirky sense of humor.

He'd ended her probation a week early with a glowing evaluation. Her clients loved her. She was in high demand. Her skill set had expanded out of necessity. She'd learned to ski and snowshoe. Two sports she'd never mastered as a Southern California girl. Allowing her job to consume her life helped time pass quickly. She hadn't spoken to Trevor, but Sam facilitated regular FaceTime chats with Emma who, at the end of every conversation, held up her bracelet and asked, "Still besties?" Her answer was always, "Yes." Each time, it brought back the sting of how things ended with Trevor.

Sam apprised her of the current situation and relayed the news of no new threats. Her replacement was being terminated and sent home. Now that Trevor's wounds had healed, he would reclaim responsibility of safeguarding himself and his family's security. He left the sad news for last when he told her he was moving on to a new assignment, out of the country. Joe would be joining him. Turns out, they'd been tracking the embedded location chips in the female who tried to kidnap Emma. The chips were activated by body heat. The ones in her clothes had gone silent, so she either ditched the clothes or the chips were discovered and destroyed, but the one in her hip was functioning and feeding them data on her whereabouts, which coincided with the known location of Boko Haram. Trevor, Sam, and Joe concluded she was a higher-level member of the guerilla group than she let on when questioned and probably the lover of one of the leaders. Otherwise, based on their reputation for the brutal treatment of women, she'd most likely have already been killed in a horrible manner.

A sense of alarm rattled Kacie's consciousness. Africa was her last mission as an active-duty Marine. Called a peace-keeping mission, it was deemed a low threat level. No one expected an ambush. She squeezed her eyes closed.

"Stay safe." She realized it was cliché but verbalizing the words made her feel better.

"We'll be okay. It's a covert operation. We're there only to do intel."

"Do me a favor?"

"Sure, Hot Stuff. Want me to take someone out?" He snorted.

"Come back," —her breath caught— "alive."

"Awe. You care about me."

"I mean it, you little shit." She disconnected the call.

****

Trevor eavesdropped on every call Emma had with Kacie. Unconcerned about what Kacie said to Emma, it was more about hearing her natural voice, lighthearted and without the strain he knew would be present if he swallowed his stubborn pride and called her. Hard as it was for him to admit, he missed her.

He had no relationship with the woman who replaced her. They barely spoke. He used Joe and Sam to forward his orders. She handled Emma with respect and professionalism, but kept it strictly business. The good news was there'd been no threats or suspicious people lurking about since the attempted kidnapping. In a final move for a return of normalcy, Trevor contacted Vince about releasing Emma's security agent. This would be her last week of employment.

He'd regained his mobility and strength. He couldn't wait for the status quo. The one thing that lingered was his need to identify who put the hit on him. The scumbag needed to pay for the chaos they had created in his life.

Last known location of the woman they tagged was in a small village on the outskirts of Bamako, in the Republic of Mali. His orders were for them to recon only and not engage, but he understood any good soldier, to feel prepared, required their weapons and gear. His father used his diplomatic resources for private transport from a local Virginia airport. Trevor had a good feeling as he waved them off from the tarmac. They'd get him answers.

When he arrived back home, the agent greeted him with a request to take Emma for ice cream at a local creamery as a goodbye gesture. His little girl loved ice cream from this family-owned shop. He mentally weighed the potential risk against Emma's need to regain her normal schedule.

"You have my okay, agent," Trevor said. "But I'm

going to tag along."

"I'll get the car," she replied.

"I'll drive," he countered. "Get Emma and meet me out front." He realized his tone with the agent was consistently brusque. He hadn't made life easy for her but she never acted defensive or challenged his authority. She carried out her duties with quiet professionalism. He planned on giving her a nice bonus on her last day. Not everyone could tolerate his brusque British behavior.

The unexpected warm weather brought out the throngs of people who also had cabin fever from the cold winter. He cruised the street in front of the Hidden House Ice Cream Parlor, but every spot was taken. Parking spaces were at a premium. He stopped in front of the shop.

"Why don't you and Emma get out here," he said to the agent. "There's a city lot a couple of blocks down the street. Freya and I will catch up."

He waited while they exited and disappeared inside the store. Then he made his way to the lot where there were plenty of available spaces. Walking for any distance remained a challenge but he no longer required the use of a cane. The sun warmed his face as he ambled along the wide sidewalk. Freya hugged his side. Bittersweet memories of Kacie entered his mind and he wondered how she was doing. The few times he'd talked to Vince, her name wasn't mentioned, which he knew was on purpose. Sam wasn't very forthcoming about her either, other than to say she was still employed at Bolton's Valor Security. Whatever conditions for continued employment Vince had laid out, and he had no doubt they were tough, Kacie had met. He missed her and not just in his bed. Her strength, her competence, and her intelligence had claimed a piece of his heart forever.

A commotion down the street drew his attention. Freya's ears went forward and she pulled ahead with urgency. He tried to assess the cause, but the sidewalk umbrellas blocked his view. The loud crack of gunfire ripped through the air. He broke into a run, drawing his weapon from the back of his waistband. Adrenaline poured through his system and numbed the pain in his leg. His only focus was on securing Emma.

Freya arrived at the scene first. He could hear her frantic bark as he approached. Outside tables were overturned and chairs upended. There was a body. *FUCK!* The young female agent lay sprawled on the concrete, blood pooled around her head. *Where's Emma?*

"Emma!" Trevor's head spun three hundred sixty degrees, his gun pointed down but his finger on the trigger. He confronted a stunned customer and commanded her to call 911. Then he dashed inside the store, scanning every corner while calling out for Emma. The store owner rushed over, clearly shaken, and stammered out the word, "Taken." He holstered his gun.

"Did you see them?" Trevor clutched the man's shoulders. "Which direction did they go?" He leaned in close to the man's face, desperate for answers. "Security cameras? Where are they?"

"We have cameras for the back but not the front." He pointed outside, his hand visibly shaking. "I was waiting on a customer but the gunshot…I looked up. The lady fell. Two masked men forced the little girl into a white panel van."

Rage ripped through Trevor. He'd hunt them down and kill them all. If they harmed one hair on Emma's head....

"Sir, the woman is deceased."

"What?"

A middle-aged woman with a calm demeanor was touching his arm. "I'm a trauma nurse. I checked her vitals and she's dead. I'm so sorry."

"Did you see what happened?"

"I saw her videoing the little girl with her phone while she was taking her first bite of ice cream. The two guys rushed the girl and when the lady fought them, one of the men shot her."

"You said phone?" Trevor's training kicked in and the rage converted into the mindset of an ambush predator.

"Yes, I think it flew out of her hand with the impact of the bullet."

The combined fire, ambulance, and police sirens blasted the air as they approached. The crowd grew as passersby stopped to observe the crime scene. He had to find the phone or it would disappear into some evidence bin. He raced outside, removed the knit cap from the agent and let Freya smell it. The dog darted around the upside-down chairs and trash strewn around, then snatched something in her teeth and brought it to him. The phone. He quickly stashed it in his pocket as the first police car screeched to a halt.

****

Trevor stepped forward and motioned one of the two police officers, a sergeant, to follow him. He directed the man to Freya, who sat motionless next the body of the dead woman. The nurse he'd spoken with earlier joined them. After he introduced himself and spelled out all his contact information along with his relationship to the victim, he deferred to the nurse as an eyewitness and slipped through the mass of curious bystanders. The second officer was securing the crime scene and herding the witnesses into the shop for questioning. He paused a short distance away and witnessed the medics cover the corpse with a white sheet. The full weight of the tragedy dropped his shoulders and buckled his knees. *There's nothing I can do for her now except exact revenge.* His mind raced against the clock.

He sped home and found the place empty. By a stroke of luck, Hazel had taken the day off and was still out. Secured in his office, he retrieved the phone left at the scene and reviewed the video. The recording started and he gasped at the sight of a happy, smiling Emma as she licked her first taste of ice cream. Tears filled his eyes and he paused the video.

I should have been there. I could have stopped them.

His stomach heaved but he pressed the play button and watched in horror as the agent valiantly battled one of the masked men, punching and kicking him. The darker skinned one drew his gun and shot her in cold blood. The phone dropped and the view went out of focus as it skidded under a table. Still recording, he heard Emma scream. One of the men cursed at the other one in Arabic. Bile rose in his throat. He recognized the West African cadence.

His first call was to Vince, who on hearing he lost an agent, bellowed a string of curse words and ended with a promise of scorched earth to find Emma.

"Do you have any idea who took her or where they went?" Vince asked.

Trevor relayed the contents of the video and emphasized how bravely Bolton's agent fought to save Emma.

"What do you need?" Vince's voice dropped into a growl.

"I need a team and fast transport to Africa to get up with my two guys already there. We can find out what intel they have. They landed in Bamako Mali."

"Done. Anything else?"

"I need Kacie."

Chapter Twenty

Out of the blue, Vince called her and, with measured words, asked her to come to his office on her day off.

Her last assignment as the primary security detail for a billionaire CEO had gone well. In fact, word of mouth amongst the rich elite kept her on continual assignment. Vince finally put his foot down and told her to take a couple of days and unwind. She'd booked a day at one of the best spas in Denver for the deluxe package. It was still early, so before she canceled, she'd find out what all the mystery was about.

Vince was waiting for her when she entered his office with an unreadable expression, but his usually pristine desk was piled high with personnel folders. His open scheduling book was filled with notes and names.

"What's going on?" She didn't wait for an invitation to sit. With her back to the wall, she selected a cushioned chair off to the side of his desk. Something was off with Vince. The hair on the back of her neck stood on end. The tension in the room was palpable.

"There's an urgent situation." He cleared his throat. "Your help has been requested."

"Please tell me this doesn't have to do with Trevor?" She pressed her lips together in a slight grimace. "Or God forbid, Emma."

"I can't tell you that." He shook his head. "Emma's

been kidnapped." He leaned forward with clasped hands and pressed them on his forehead. "I'm putting together a team and Trevor specifically requested you." He peered up at her. "I can't force you to go but—"

"I'm in. I'll get my kit. What is our go time?"

"Glad to hear it. We leave tonight at twenty-two hundred on a private jet I arranged to borrow from one of our clients. I'll be at Rocky Mountain Metropolitan Airport to see you and the guys off, but I'm remaining here to monitor the operation."

"Why so late? I can be mission ready in two hours."

"Trevor is flying here. He's coming on the Op along with Gil as the communications specialist and two other special operators familiar with Africa. Sam and Joe are already in Mali."

"I understand. Don't worry. I can handle it." *Could she? I must stay mission-focused for Emma. The last place on earth I want to travel to is Mali.* "I assume Trevor will brief the team on the flight over?"

"Yes, you know Trevor. He'll have complete mission details ready when he boards the flight." He sighed. "I need you to call him ahead of his arrival here." He tapped the end of his pen on the desk. "Clear the air. Say anything that might compromise the mission if left unspoken. Get your house in order, if you catch my drift."

"Loud and clear, sir." She stood. "My phone's in the car. I'll call him straight away. See you tonight." She made a beeline to her car and snatched her phone from her purse. *I hope and pray Emma was wearing her bracelet.* She scrolled through her apps and found the GPS location finder she'd installed after she gave

Emma the bracelet. With her eyes closed, she silently said a prayer and opened the app. The red dot associated with Emma moved but the location was undetectable. Was she in the air? The GPS relied on satellites, but once in the air, its accuracy faltered, the signal weakened and far less precise than on solid ground. Still, it was a lead.

She plugged her phone into the charger and located Trevor on her contact list. The call would be a double-edged sword. She dreaded the potential admonishment from Trevor for not being there, which sounded harsher in his British accent. She doubted she could have prevented the kidnapping any better than the agent on duty but guilt was easy for her and she'd wear the full weight of it if it facilitated the success of the mission. She hoped her admission she'd imbedded a tracker on Emma's bracelet would serve to balance his need for a rebuke of her decision to leave.

"Kacie," he said, followed by a soft curse. "Thank God."

"Trevor, I'm so sorry." She paused. "We'll get her back."

"So, you'll join the hunt?"

"Yes, but we should have a talk to clear the air before you arrive out here."

"I can't lose her, Kacie." His voice choked. "The past doesn't matter. I just want my little girl home. You know Emma and you served in Africa, specifically Mali. Your help will be invaluable."

She sensed Trevor was hyper-focused on Emma and wasn't addressing his grief over the lost agent or their breakup. Vince expected her to be squared away before the start of the operation and she intended to comply. The promise propelled her to dig in.

"Vince told me your agent got killed trying to protect Emma. I regret not being there."

"I don't." He snapped his reply.

She clutched the steering wheel and braced herself for the avalanche of recrimination.

"The agent was shot in cold blood because I was parking my car two blocks away and not there to back her up. If you'd been there, no doubt it would have been you lying in a pool of blood on the ground. I'm sick the agent lost her life, but it would have destroyed me if you were the one with a bullet in your head."

She'd misjudged Trevor and underestimated the extent of his feelings. This wasn't the conversation she thought they'd have. Her mind spun while she worked to gain control of her spiraling emotions. Stunned by his admission, Kacie struggled to get the conversation back on track and fulfill her promise to Vince, but Trevor continued.

"Emma was kidnapped because of me. Once we arrive in Mali, I have no idea how we'll find my daughter." His voice lowered. "I plan to offer myself in trade for Emma. It's me those assholes want. It's me they're going to get."

"That might not be the only solution," she said with conviction. "Was Emma wearing the bracelet I gave her?"

"That's your concern?" He spit out the question.

"I put a tracker in one of the dark stones next to the nameplate. It's active."

****

"You did what?" His body shivered from the shock of conflict between hope and anger. "In what world is it okay you put a tracker on my daughter without asking me?"

"The security world." She heaved a sigh. "I did it on impulse with no intention of malice or of bypassing your parental authority. And to be honest, Trevor, we weren't on the best of terms."

His temper cooled. Hope prevailed. As usual, Kacie's instincts were spot-on. Her keen ability to forecast the unpredictable was impressive.

"You're right. I made it hard for you but thank goodness you disregarded my obtuse behavior and did the right thing. I owe you an apology."

"You don't owe me anything. I broke the most basic rule of security by getting too attached to my charges. The last few months have taught me how to perform my duties with detachment but still care about the safety of my clients. Vince gave me the option of turning this assignment down, because of our past, but I didn't hesitate. Emma is important to me and I'd wade waist-deep in Tijuana sewage to get her back home."

"Are you crying?"

"Yes." She sniffled, then laughed. "All this time I worked so hard to prove my detached professionalism but none of it matters now. All that matters is Emma."

"Because of your instincts in placing the tracker, we're going to get her back and kill the bastards who took her. The fact that you're alive, that you feel pain, remorse, and love is not a detriment, Kacie. They are the qualities of a true warrior."

"So, we're good?" she hesitated, then added, "enough to work on this op together?"

"Right as rain. Boarding the plane now." He panted as he used the handrails to ascend two stairs at a time with an eighty-pound backpack filled with equipment. "See you in a few hours. Keep your eye on the tracker movement."

"Eyes clued. Hey, Trev, thanks for coming to us. Despite you having to crisscross the US, it gives us time to fully assemble the team and get them kitted up. We'll be ready by the time you get here. Hopefully, we can catch some shut eye over the Atlantic."

"Either way, I'll be locked and loaded." He ended the call.

Chapter Twenty-One

Somewhere Over the Atlantic Ocean

The flight over the Atlantic in the Gulfstream G650ER was smooth and uneventful. After Trevor briefed the team on the kidnapping and the intel Joe and Sam had gleaned from their groundwork, Kacie read in everyone on Emma's tracker and its current whereabouts. Still hours before they landed in Mali, the snores of the men, accustomed to sleeping on long-distance flights, could be heard throughout the large cabin of the private jet. Kacie leaned her seat back and closed her eyes.

"Is this seat taken?" Trevor asked.

She recognized his voice but eased open one eye and indicated with a wave of her hand to sit, then shuttered her lid.

Freya's wet nose touched her fingers. She sensed what the dog wanted and rubbed her head but stayed in her reclined position.

"We're going to be landing in a couple of hours. Could we talk before the guys wake up? Trevor asked.

"Sure." Kacie raised her seatback and scanned his face. "I like the beard. It suits you."

"Thanks." He rubbed his chin. "You didn't comment earlier when I arrived in Denver, so I was wondering."

"Nervous about the mission?"

"Nervous? No." He shook his head.

"Amped up?" she asked with a tilt of her head.

"Yes, but I wondered...." He stopped and glanced around the plane. "Are you seeing anyone?"

"You mean one of these guys?" She nodded her head toward the rear of the plane.

"Well, yes, but also generally."

"All of them." She watched his cheeks above the beard line turn pink, then chuckled, "Kidding. I wanted to see if you'd blush."

"Bloody devilish woman."

"I'm not seeing anyone," she said flatly.

The seats were close enough together that she could observe the pulse throbbing in his neck. Neither one of them gave any ground but kept eye contact until an announcement from the pilot blared over the speaker, saying they had entered African airspace. The hue of Trevor's bright, cobalt blue eyes sparked with a darker, deeper shade but he maintained his focus. The heat from his gaze stirred memories of his touch. Her breath quickened. She lost touch with her environment and was vaguely aware when another passenger commented as he passed their seats. Trevor smoothed his hand over her thigh and her legs involuntarily parted. Her brain scrambled to shift her thoughts away from steamy nights in his bed. If she didn't do something right away, she'd be dragged willingly into the bathroom where they'd join the mile high club with honors.

She broke the gaze and checked her watch. *I took one for the team that time.*

"I'm surprised but happy." Trevor lifted his hand and put it on the armrest.

"About what?" She couldn't remember what she'd said.

"That you're not seeing anyone," he said with a laugh.

"Oh, that." She tried to sound nonchalant. "No time. My job has kept me too busy for dating." No way she'd admit he was the real reason she'd been celibate. She rested her hand on her cheek. "You?"

"I think you know the answer to that question!"

"Well, here we are, Mr. Marlowe. Together but apart." She glanced out the window at the city lights in the distance. "We're getting close to our insertion point. We should do an equipment check before we land."

"Agreed." He stood and moved into the aisle. "Want help rousting the team?"

"Sure, but no cold water in the face or ice down the back. I'm familiar with your special operator tricks."

"Kill joy." He snorted.

The banter was back. Their relationship was on the mend, although it might never resume where they left off. The ease between them would help with mission success. She was ready to face the demons she'd left on the battlefield in Mali. Squared away and prepared for Emma's rescue, she viewed Trevor's command presence as he rallied the other operators.

The tracker, still active, had become stationary in a city called Mopti. She suspected the red dot to be the location, most likely an abandoned building, where the enemy combatants stashed Emma. They'd have to move with speed and precision to pull off the rescue.

Mindful of her last deployment to Africa, she brought cash and silver for bribes. Although most African governments were allied with the United States due to the large sums of aid handed out, the locals could sometimes be hostile toward outsiders. Allied with the guerrilla groups out of fear or payoffs, local officials wouldn't hesitate to alert them to the presence of Americans who didn't arrive on tour buses.

Step by step, she checked her equipment. She verified the bags of coins and rolls of bills were where she'd stuffed them in a side pocket of her backpack. Ten thousand dollars were all donated by an anonymous benefactor in case they had to bribe their way out of the country. She said a silent prayer and crossed her heart the mission wouldn't come to such a dire circumstance.

Chapter Twenty-Two

Bamako, Mali

Trevor opened the shade of the window and peered down at the semiarid landscape filled with scrubby vegetation. The morning sun broke over the large escarpment rising above the Niger River as the plane circled the capital and largest city of Mali.

In recent years, Bamako had seen significant urban development, with the construction of modern buildings, shopping malls, and infrastructure projects aimed at improving the quality of life for its residents, most of whom lived below the poverty level for Africans.

Bamako was chosen as their entry point into the country due to its larger size. A group of white travelers with large backpacks, bulky duffle bags and gun cases wouldn't stand out as much here. There was also the availability of a private airstrip for non-commercial jets located within the boundaries of the international airport, safeguarding them against nosy customs agents.

Joe and Sam, already on the ground, tracked the female kidnapper to a nearby village where she visited a mosque. She left alone and took a cab to the airport, where she bought a ticket on a small commercial airline to Mopti.

The two men greased the lines with the diplomatic paperwork his father provided by calling in a plethora of favors. Their designated status was an agricultural mission. It applied in the loosest of terms.

Trevor's friend, Jack, would also be there to greet them. Still serving in the SAS, he was currently deployed to Mali and had his thumb on the pulse of the country. He had friends high up in the Mali military in case they got wind of the upcoming, unauthorized deployment of Americans in their country. Jack had assured him good bourbon and smokes served as an acceptable bribe for most of the intel he required for his current assignment. Passive surveillance on the assault of vermin the military leaders wanted out of their country would be a no-brainer.

He and Jack had survived several firefights together in Afghanistan, and he trusted the soldier with his life. You can get a good gauge of a man's character when the bullets start whizzing over your head and Jack's was exemplary.

Jack couldn't legally join them on the ground in their off-books mission, but he'd secured transportation for them via a British military hop to Mopti. The Chinook HC4 helicopter waited for them on a private farm a few miles away. Once in Mopti, he'd be on standby in case they got their asses in a sling, but couldn't be an official part of the op.

"We're ready to deplane," Kacie said, with a light touch on his arm. "What's on your mind?"

"Mission success," he said grabbing his pack from the overhead. "The wheels should be greased for us to board our hop to Mopti." When he reached the exit, the glare of the sun hit his face with blazing intensity. He pulled a pair of aviators from his front shirt pocket and slid them on, then made his way down the stairs. Kacie exited behind him, followed by the rest of the team.

"Shit, it's hot." He swiped the sheen off his forehead and hefted his bag into a more comfortable position. "I need a hat."

"Here you go," Kacie said and withdrew a baseball cap from her back pocket.

"San Diego?" Trevor glanced at the monogrammed bill and popped it on his head.

"Well, it's better than my other cap which has 'infidel' stenciled on the front."

Trevor wanted to tell her how much it meant to him she was on the team but stifled the remark when he noticed Jack head straight for her, a familiar leer on his face. *Here we go. Pass interference.*

"Hey, brother." He cut off Jack's approach with a huge grin.

"Good to see you, Trevor, you fucking door-kicker." His weathered face crinkled with a smile as he wrapped his muscular arms around Trevor and lifted him off the ground.

"Ditch the cuddle, mate."

"Only if you introduce me to the babe," Jack said, tipping his cap at Kacie.

"Kacie, this is Jack."

"Pleasure, ma'am." Jack loosened his hold on Trevor and stuck out his hand.

"Transportation, Jack. Nice to meet you." Kacie clasped his outstretched hand and used her free hand to place on his chest as he stepped forward. "Having one SAS asshole in my life is quite enough."

"Oh, sorry, man." Jack's head ping-ponged from Kacie to Trevor. "But good on you, bro."

"Let me introduce you to the rest of the team,"

Trevor said, ignoring the innuendo, but lifted by her words. Hope he and Kacie had a future together served as armor against the doubt he'd make it out alive if the only option for getting Emma back was to surrender himself. They were about to be plunged into the dark world owned by a nest of snakes.

****

All roads led to Mopti. Kacie checked the tracker for what seemed like the tenth time in the last five minutes. She feared the enemy combatants would remove the bracelet as a trade item. She knew from experience barter was a way of life in Africa. If they inspected the one black rectangular bead and discovered the tracker, they'd kill Emma and flee. She kept this concern close to the chest, but a renewed sense of urgency niggled her mind.

With the team loaded, the pilot of the Chinook helicopter lifted off and swung northeast toward Mopti. Situated three hundred and ninety-one miles northeast of Bamako, the estimated time of arrival was two-and one-half hours or noon, local time.

Jack turned out to be quite resourceful. He'd arranged for a secure base camp where they'd recheck their equipment and check the maps for all extraction points. Sam and Joe would reconnoiter the city and locate the building where Emma's tracker continued to ding. With any luck, the female agent's tracker would lead to the same place.

Pre-encounter nerves were always a part of a dangerous mission even for the most seasoned operator. Hers rattled like an old jalopy. The last mission she went on ended in a blood bath. She unsnapped her harness, scooted over to Trevor and grabbed his hand.

The noise in the helicopter made it difficult to talk but she mouthed, "You okay?"

"I'm feeling perfectly diabolical." He spoke directly in her ear while he squeezed her hand.

She'd seen this version of Trevor before when he transformed from a proper British gentleman to an ambush predator. Chameleon described the single factor separating regular military and Special Forces. Capable of combat with twenty kills one week and then home to play legos with their two-year-old after their tour of duty ended. She nodded and gave him a thumbs-up, but when she started to scoot away, he pressed their intertwined hands over his heart. His face wore the look of determined resignation. A chill shivered through her body. Did he still have the idea he might have to sacrifice himself for Emma? Didn't he understand it was a lose-lose proposition? The Boka Haram bosses would behead him and sell Emma to the highest bidder.

The chopper circled the field while the team checked the grounds below for any farm workers or curious townspeople who'd wandered to the outskirts. Once cleared, the pilot made a smooth landing and waited for everyone to disembark before lifting off.

Joe and Sam stayed by themselves for most of the trip, but when they formed a circle to coordinate assignments, Sam strolled next to her.

"How was the flight over?"

"You mean with Trevor?" She huffed "We're on the same page. It's about finding Emma."

"I'm surprised your boss allowed you to come but I'm glad to have you on the team."

"Thanks. I volunteered." She shoved her hands in her pants pocket. "Does Joe hate me for leaving? He hasn't smiled at me or said two words since I got here."

"Joe? Oh hell no." He pointed to Joe. "Honestly, he needs to get laid. It's all about work with him, although he did say this was a particular suck-fest."

"This whole thing does suck and I know it's eating Trevor alive wondering what those goons are doing to his little girl."

"You're the expert in hostage negotiation. What do you think our chances are?"

"None if we try to negotiate. Slim to none if you don't get a move on before nightfall and confirm the location." She handed him her phone and showed him the tracker app. "We'll have comms operational within the hour and be able to communicate via my headset." She pointed toward the ground transportation Jack had arranged. "Get your ass in gear."

"Thanks for noticing my ass." Sam winked, turned on a dime, and disappeared into the mass of men and equipment.

****

Nightfall arrived none too soon for the eager group of men. Kacie's gaze turned toward the sky. The gibbous moon, surrounded by a smattering of bright stars, offered enough ambient light for the team to navigate the dirt road into town without their tactical flashlights. A few yards outside the perimeter of town, the team lowered their night vision goggles, fanned out, and assumed their respective assault positions. Trevor, as point man, led Kacie and Gil, the communications guy, to the rendezvous point where Sam and Joe waited behind a row of warehouses on the South side of town. Fortunately, this side of town was industrial and lacked the curious eyes of human traffic prevalent on the North side of town. Police presence also appeared scarce.

"Sitrep," Trevor said. He bent on one knee.

Kacie, flat against the wall of the closet building, scanned the area, rifle at the ready.

"There's been activity. We followed our specious female agent to this site. She arrived an hour ago, accompanied by two masked men armed with automatic weapons."

"Any sign of Emma?" Trevor asked.

Sam held out Kacie's phone with the tracker app open. A red dot blinked at the back of the warehouse. Trevor grabbed the phone and stared at the screen.

"We're going in." His voice, low and guttural, set the team in motion.

Chapter Twenty-Three

"There's a problem," said Joe. "The place is a fortress with the front door as the only viable way in and out. Iron bars cover all the windows. There is a back door but a locked metal grate compromises access. Two heavily armed men guard both the front and the back."

Trevor clenched his fists. Taking out the guards wouldn't be difficult. He was an expert with a knife, as were Joe and Sam. The bigger concern was they had apparently stumbled upon headquarters for the Mali faction of Boko Haram. His team was comprised of seasoned Special Forces soldiers, but the possibility they might be confronted by a much larger force than anticipated gave him pause. Rules of engagement didn't exist within uncivilized groups of drug-crazed insurgents driven by hatred of western culture. It would come down to kill or be killed.

"Thermal breaching is an option for the back grate," Joe said. "Do you know if a torch was part of our equipment package?"

"Yes," Kacie said, "a cutting torch was included. One of the guys on the east perimeter has it along with a sledgehammer."

"Cutting will take too long for entry," Trevor said. "We don't know the size of the enemy force inside or the number of outliers who could roll in within minutes of being texted."

"What do you suggest?" Joe asked.

"We blow the locks off the grate and the back door with a shotgun."

"A blast from a shotgun will be loud and draw unwanted attention." Joe countered.

"Not if we have a prior distraction go boom at the front door."

"An explosive breach?" Kacie asked.

"Yes. One big enough to blow the door off its hinges and smoke anyone close by." He swept his hands in a wide circle. "Radio our guys to assume their positions. Tell the men doing overwatch to position from the rear of the warehouse roof next door and cover our exfil." He nodded to Gil and stood. "Joe and I are going to check out the back door."

Trevor pulled out a long knife from a sheath and pointed it at Joe, who slid his knife out and touched the sharp point. They'd take out the guards on the rear door and hide their bodies.

Gil touched the 'on' button on his headset and sent orders for the team they were a go for the mission. He listened for a minute, then gave a thumbs-up to Trevor who nodded and ducked out from the secure position behind the nearby warehouse with Joe close behind. Using hand signals, he indicated for Sam and Kacie to keep watch, then disappeared into the darkness.

Trevor returned with apprehension and an unorthodox plan. There was a direct way into the room where Emma was being held. An exhaust and intake air vent had been installed in the ceiling of the room with access from the roof. It required a lithe figure to slide through the opening and his men were all too bulked up, but Kacie would fit. It was a risky move. One that could get her killed. The only other option was storming the place, guns blazing, which could get Emma, along with some of his men, killed.

If I didn't have feelings for Kacie, would I be reluctant about the decision to send her in? I doubt it. For the first time, Trevor understood the turmoil he'd put Kacie through. Truly understood how much pain he'd caused her. *I'm a first-class lout.*

"What do you need from me, Trevor?" Kacie tucked her long ponytail under her cap.

"It's a big ask." He squeezed his eyes shut for a second. "You'd be the first one in, without any support."

"I'll do it." Her eyes widened. "For Emma."

****

Kacie stripped down to bra and panties. Trevor fitted the bullet-proof vest over her head and tightened the straps. She tossed the cotton t-shirt he offered over her head and tugged on a pair of cargo pants. He threaded her bowie knife onto her canvas web belt and knelt to tie the required double rawhide around her thigh. Her breath caught as his head brushed her crotch. He stood and handed her a 9mm gun, which she secured in her Kydex holster.

"Stay safe," he said as he positioned the headset on her head.

Kacie, Trevor, and Joe advanced to the warehouse while Sam and his team proceeded to their position by the front of the building where the sniper had already eliminated the two guards.

"Timing will be tight," Trevor said to Kacie as he boosted her onto the tin roof. "As soon as you have

Emma and you're clear of the back door—"

"I've got this. I say, *GO*."

She reached the vent in a crouched scuttle and peered through the plexiglass top. A dim light shone in the room. Her heart thudded as she viewed Emma gagged, blindfolded and tied to a wooden, straight-backed chair. "She's alive and alone," Kacie whispered into her headset. "Ready when you are."

Working quickly, she unscrewed the bolts holding the cover in place, ripped out the screen underneath and waited for the blast.

The double tap sounded seconds before the blast shook the entire building as the front door blew off its hinges. Gunshots rang out. Panicked voices shouted orders. She dropped feet first through the narrow hole and ran to Emma. When she lifted off the blindfold, Emma struggled to get free. Kacie held up her index finger to her lips and removed the dirty cloth used as a gag. She retrieved her knife to cut the zip ties binding Emma's ankles and wrists, but when she knelt to cut them, she noticed the barbaric bastards had tattooed the six-year-old's wrist.

Enraged by the realization they had no intention of a ransom or a trade for Trevor but planned to sell the little girl, she sliced the binds with a fevered intensity.

Freed, Emma threw herself into Kacie's arms. Her little body shook. Kacie held her tight for a few seconds, stunned by how close they'd come to never seeing her again.

"Your daddy is outside waiting." Emma continued to cling to Kacie, who said 'go' into her microphone with quiet but firm conviction.

As Kacie hunched over Emma, prepared for the

shotgun blast, the internal door opened with a bang and a brute of a man rushed in brandishing a long, curved knife. He yelled in French, then lunged at her. She dodged the blade and pushed Emma behind the chair. He dove again, this time nicking her arm. The first shotgun blast rang out. Aware help was coming, she charged him, and snap-kicked him in the groin. He stumbled backward but regained his balance and hurtled toward Emma, screaming. Kacie advanced, and with a throat strike, crushed his larynx. He gasped for air, grabbed his throat, then collapsed in a heap on the floor. The second blast shattered the lock on the door. Seconds later, Trevor bolted through the open space, with Joe close behind.

Trevor ran to Emma and scooped her into his arms. She buried her head in his neck and sobbed. He patted her on the back, while his face, painted with relief, lifted skyward.

"Guys, we need to exfil now." Joe nodded toward the sharp bark of continued gunfire from the other side of the warehouse.

"Joe, take point. Kacie, rearguard," Trevor said. "Sniper is on the roof and Sam's out front with his guys drawing fire from the remaining insurgents."

Joe raised his rifle and stepped to the door. Trevor, carrying Emma, fell in behind Joe. As he passed Kacie, he touched her bloodied arm. A flash of fury crossed his face when he realized the depth of the gash.

"I'm okay." She scoffed at her arm. "Let's get Emma home."

Chapter Twenty-Four

McLean, Virginia

Trevor awakened from a fitful sleep. They'd been home a week and although he tried his damnedest to return life to as normal as possible for Emma, she refused to go outside the house, to step in the fenced backyard, even with Freya. Her silence about the incident worried him. Usually a curious child with an inquiring mind, she regularly asked questions about any new exposure or experience. Not this time. He perceived her retreating from life.

The medic, who was part of the team, checked her out thoroughly on the plane ride home. He reported no sign of serious injury, torture or abuse but said her clammy skin, enlarged pupils and rapid pulse indicated a stage of shock which he treated her for with standard protocol. The tattoo, upon examination, turned out to be done with metal ink which was difficult to remove but wasn't painful when applied. It would eventually wear off. His final comment after they disembarked back in the United States, suggested Trevor seek professional help for Emma for possible PTSD.

His father flew back to the United States from his overseas diplomatic assignment as soon as Trevor called him with the news his granddaughter was safe. He brought her crayons and pads of unlined paper in case she wanted to draw pictures about what happened.

He also brought chocolates and picture books, all her favorites, but instead of bouncing into his arms at first sight, she greeted him with an understated thank you, a smile and a half-hearted hug. He didn't act disappointed but gave her space and told her she was his favorite. The gesture usually got a huge giggle as they both understood she was his *only* grandchild, but this time she simply nodded.

Having his father home helped him cope. The senior Marlowe vowed to stay as long as needed. Through his diplomatic channels he'd received word the Mali military had pursued the remnants of the terrorist faction and either killed or arrested all members. He also mentioned the news media had picked up the story and suggested they limit Emma's exposure to repetitive news reports about the traumatic event.

Trevor entered the kitchen to bring Hazel up to date on the news his father had shared and found her baking Emma's favorite chocolate cupcakes with sprinkles on top.

"She'll devour those cupcakes, Hazel." He swiped his finger in the bowl of icing and licked the sweet chocolate off the end. "Mmmm. You outdid yourself."

"Emma picked at her lunch, said her stomach hurt and asked permission to go to her room." She pursed her lips. "At this point, I'm not worried about vegetables."

"I agree. I'll go check on her."

He found her curled up in a fetal position inside her closet. His emotions seesawed between rage and grief. Seventy hours of hell transformed his precocious, cheerful daughter into a frightened, withdrawn mouse.

He and his team had successfully eliminated the threat but in her mind, the terror lived on.

The sadness in Emma's eyes crushed him. There was a distinct hollowness in her voice and the enthusiastic giggle that previously emanated throughout the house had disappeared. She constantly touched the tattoo on her wrist, but as soon as Trevor noticed, she quickly hid her hand.

"You want to tell me about the tattoo?" he asked in a soft tone. He sat on the floor in a relaxed lotus position.

"I don't like it." She rubbed her wrist and frowned. "I want it off." Her face flushed red.

"It will come off, little one, but I'll look into how to make it disappear faster." His throat tightened with emotion. Anger was a good sign and she was talking.

"Why did the lady put the number on me?" She stared at the black numerals on the inside of her wrist.

"Because she's a very bad person. She's gone now and you'll never see her again."

"I want Kacie's bracelet but I lost it." She whimpered. "I was afraid the bad men would take it, so I tucked the whole thing inside the arm of my jacket."

"That's my smart girl." His heart broke for Emma. He wanted to wrap her in his arms and never let go, but he kept his tone calm and low key. "You remember the nice doctor on the plane who talked to you on the way home?" She nodded. "He took it off while he was examining you but he gave it to me. I have it."

"I want to wear it." She held up her wrist. "And make these numbers disappear."

No way he'd disabuse her of the idea Kacie's gift wasn't magical. The bracelet would help camouflage the hideous tattoo. The expectant look on her face was all he needed.

"It's in my office. I'll go get it." He scrambled up. Emma flinched and drew back at his sudden movement.

"Want to come with me?" He held out his hand and she clutched his palm. With a gentle pull, he brought her to a standing position. She brushed off nonexistent dirt from her shirt and pants. A single tear trickled down her cheek.

"Can I sleep in your room again tonight, Daddy?" She peered up at him with a wide-eyed expression. "On the pallet you fixed, next to Freya."

"Whatever you want, dear girl."

"I want to talk to Kacie."

****

Kacie returned home a reluctant hero. Gil praised her bravery to Vince who repeated it at the staff meeting along with quotes from Trevor in his final debrief. All the attention for simply doing her job made her uncomfortable. She shifted from foot to foot and clasped her hands behind her back as the clapping turned into a standing ovation. When asked to say a few words, she was brief and thanked the men for their outstanding teamwork, unwavering determination and topflight skills.

Vince called her into his office a week later and offered her a promotion. She'd be a trainer for all the newbies. Quite a compliment, as these newbies were veteran war fighters from all branches of the military, some with years of experience. She'd be responsible for grooving them in on all of Bolton Valor's procedures and testing their readiness for an assignment. Not only was the job a leap in pay, but she wouldn't have to travel outside the area. She pinched herself.

Vince also awarded her three paid days off to relax and consider the offer. She honestly didn't need to think about accepting an offer for a dream job but decided it'd be a good time to redeem the spa certificate she'd left unused. Her arm, still bandaged, did require stitches, which the medic sutured on the flight back, but the massage therapist could work around the inconvenience. She left the office with a spring in her step. Her road to redemption had proven difficult and full of potholes but rescuing Emma and returning her safely home with no casualties had erased the shame, blame and regret from her earlier deployment. The loss of three of her men on her first trip to Africa would forever be imprinted in her memory, but no longer haunted her dreams. She'd reunited with happiness like a long-lost cousin.

Once in her car, she gunned the engine and headed for her little slice of heaven on the outskirts of Winding Creek. Her renter had moved out and she'd settled in. It felt good to have her routine back.

She looked forward to the drive home. The surrounding mountain peaks, still covered in snow, rose with majestic splendor as she sped closer. Spring closed in on the region with the fresh fragrance of native foliage and daffodils blooming alongside the road. She pressed the button and lowered the windows, inhaling a deep breath.

Her phone rang and cut into her serenity. She glanced at the screen of her hands-free system. *Trevor.* When they dropped him and Emma off at the airport in Virginia, they promised to stay in touch, but neither one of them had initiated a phone call or text. *Why didn't I call?*

"Trevor, hi. How are things? How's Emma?"

"Emma's not good." He choked. "I need your help."

"Oh no. I'm so sorry I haven't called." She felt like an insensitive heel. Emma had been quiet on the flight back and clung close to Freya and her father but she thought the behavior was normal considering what she'd been through. On her way off the plane, she hugged Kacie and said thank you. Emma appeared exhausted, but Kacie considered her one of the most resilient human beings she'd ever met. She understood it would take a while to recover from the trauma but figured time at home surrounded by familiar, loving adults would go a long way in healing her.

"You have your life, I understand."

"What's going on?" His tone of resignation alarmed her. "What can I do to help?"

"Emma asked to talk to you."

"Of course. I want to talk to her. I miss her. Honesty, I would have called but I didn't want to interfere with any therapy she was receiving." She clucked her tongue. "Be a reminder of what happened."

"We haven't gotten a therapist yet."

"Oh. I thought…." She pulled into her driveway and turned off the engine. "Never mind what I thought."

"She'll need counseling, but we determined the best thing for her in the present was basic routine and familiar faces. We're at a critical point right now. She barely eats or talks and won't go outside, even in our fenced yard and even with Freya. My dad is here but she's not engaged."

"Jesus, Trevor. You think she'll talk to me?"

"Yes. I do. She also asked for her bracelet you gave her, so it's important."

"Okay. Good starting point. Hey, I'm home. How about we FaceTime?"

"Good idea. I'll get Emma."

"You got it. Hey, Trev. I'm going to let Emma decide how she wants this conversation to go. I admit I'm not an expert on children but it seems she needs to feel in control of her life in some small way. If she stares at the screen and doesn't talk, okay with me. I'll smile back while I twiddle my thumbs. I want her to feel in control.

Trevor didn't answer. Her screen showed he had ended the call. Kacie grabbed her laptop, sprinted into the house, and wasted no time setting up the FaceTime link in her web browser. Then, she held her breath and waited.

Chapter-Twenty-Five

Emma's sweet little face stared at the screen. Her tangled red hair fell around her shoulders, and the dark circles under her eyes revealed a despondent state. Her blank expression didn't throw Kacie off. She'd already decided it didn't matter what Emma said or did or didn't say or do. What mattered was Kacie showed up.

After about five minutes, Emma pointed to the beaded bracelet on her wrist and smiled. Kacie took the cue and smiled back as she pointed to her similar bracelet. Trevor sat to the side of the screen but was still visible. His ashen complexion exposed his lack of sleep, sun, and proper food. *Poor guy. I feel for him. He's sitting at rock bottom.*

Emma sat up straighter in her chair. She reached for a hairbrush on her desk and tugged through her tangles. Trevor leaned forward, his brow furrowed, but Kacie skewered him with a 'don't' help look. She texted him under the table with the message, *—I've got this.—*

Kacie removed her brush from her knapsack, and with short, smooth strokes, ran it through her hair. She used her fingers to thread through imaginary tangles. Emma mimicked the motion. They continued until Emma ran the brush through her hair in a fluid sweep.

Kacie's study of the most successful therapy for children revealed mimicry got the best results.

Delighted to witness Emma's response, she placed her brush on the desk and gave Emma two thumbs-up. A smile eased across the little girl's face as she laid her brush down. Kacie thought Trevor might jump up and cartwheel around the room. Instead, his eyes conveyed his happiness.

This was their first encounter since returning home, and Kacie thought it best to use a gradient approach. Art had been a favorite activity they shared when Kacie served as her security and, hoping it still would be, she produced two sheets of white unlined paper along with a box of colored pencils. She drew a large question mark on the first sheet and held it up for Emma?

Emma glanced at her father, who scrambled to retrieve the coloring book and crayons Kacie had given her. Emma squirmed in her chair in apparent anticipation until he handed her a plain white sheet of paper, along with a box of crayons. She withdrew the red one and with intense concentration drew on the paper. Then she hoisted it in front of her face so Kacie could view the image. Kacie blinked back tears and crossed her legs like a vice, to keep her emotions in check. Her inner voice screamed hallelujah but when she spoke, it was simple.

"Ditto, little one."

The broad smile on Emma's face transformed into a wide yawn.

"I'd like to take a nap, Daddy." She stretched her arms over her head. "Can we talk again, Kacie?"

"Whenever you like." Kacie's body vibrated with a sense of hope. It was a start. A small portion of the suffering in the beautiful six-year-old mind had been snuffed out.

"Tomorrow, please." She glanced at her father, who nodded. "Do you think Hazel has any chocolate chip cookies left? I'm hungry."

"I bet she has one or two. Let's go check." He mouthed a thank you to Kacie and tapped his fist to his heart.

"Sleep tight, Emma," Kacie said with a smile and a wave. She disconnected the video call, then face-planted on the desk. Uncontrolled sobs shook her body. The connection with Emma was undeniable. She missed her and as much as she tried to deny it, she longed for Trevor's embrace, but there was no going back.

****

After a week of daily talks with Kacie, Trevor noticed a marked improvement in his daughter. Her nightmares were less frequent, and her appetite had returned. His one big worry was her unwillingness to go outside of the house. She preferred sticking close to Hazel in the kitchen or coloring on the floor in his office while he worked.

Prior to the threat and all the ensuing chaos and required security, his father arranged her enrollment in a private school which catered to the children of diplomats. At the time, she was excited to attend, but when he asked if she'd like to resume her studies, she flatly refused. After discussing the problem with his father, they researched home school programs and found one that would give Emma credits. At least she wouldn't fall behind.

To interest Emma in going outdoors, his father purchased a state-of-the-art playground with two slides, a climbing wall, and a fireman's pole, and installed it in the backyard. After three days of staring at the monstrosity through the kitchen window, she asked to go outside but only if Freya, Hazel and he went with her. That night, in a breakthrough, she described the playground to Kacie in detail and ended with the notion it would have been more fun if she'd been there.

Trevor recognized a key component in Emma's progress toward recovery was Kacie's involvement. He asked her if they could have a private conversation soon. He had an idea he wanted to propose. She'd agreed to talk after work. The idea of asking her to come back to Virginia seemed crazy but it was exactly what he planned to do.

"Is now a good time?" Trevor asked, adjusting his head piece when she answered the call.

"Good as any," she said. "Is Emma okay?"

"Better." He hesitated. "Thanks to your willingness to help."

"Like I wouldn't do anything for her?" She huffed.

"I'm glad you said that. I have a proposal which might sound outlandish but I'm out of other options."

"Okay," she answered, her tone edged with caution.

They weren't getting off to a good start. He could sense her apprehension. Although he was present for the talks between Emma and Kacie, he and Kacie hadn't said two words to each other about what was happening in their individual lives. Was she happy? Did she still work for Bolton Valor's Security and Investigations? Was she seeing anyone?

"Sorry, small talk isn't my forte." He sighed. "Let's back this up. For starters, how's work? I assume you're still working for Valor?"

"As a matter of fact, yes, and it's going great."

"Do you have to travel much, or do they give you local assignments?"

"I'm permanently stationed at headquarters."

The news took him by surprise. Did she get grounded? Vince wasn't stupid. No way after the success of the Mali mission. A promotion?

"Whoa. You got promoted?"

"Yes. It's my dream job." Her voice rose. "I'm the trainer for all the new guys. It's exactly where I want to be."

What was he thinking? That he could simply rip her from her life and ask her to come back to Virginia. The fact she cared about Emma didn't mean she owed him anything. He'd been so interiorized into his own problem, he foolishly assumed she would be, too.

"What was your proposal, Trevor?" she asked.

"It was a hairbrained scheme." He kept his voice light, but his pulse raced like a downhill toboggan with no brakes.

"You? Having anything hairbrained is laughable. You're the most deliberate man I've ever met."

"I was going to propose you move back here for a while until Emma recovers." *There, I said it.* "But after hearing about your promotion, I realize it's not reality."

"Oh, Trevor. I'm glad I'm helping Emma, but me coming there would only give her another reason to stay inside. I have a counterproposal."

"Well, that's a relief. You could have called me a selfish cad and I would have deserved it."

"OMG. You're such a Brit." Kacie laughed. "I've done research on the most effective therapies for children recovering from traumatic events, and I found one I think Emma would participate in. She'd go outside for this one."

"What is it?"

"There are organizations that use horses and horseback riding as therapy for veterans with PTSD and they have been hugely successful."

"She loves horses but she's only six, Kacie."

"I found one for children out here in Denver. Of course, if you located a suitable outfit in Virginia—"

"I'm in."

Chapter Twenty-Six

What the hell did I get myself into? Her mind buzzed with the consequences of having Trevor in Denver. Their focus would be on helping Emma recover, but could she keep it exclusively to a single goal? Deep down, did she want a totally platonic relationship with him?

A relationship with him would always be complicated. His injuries were healed enough to be active duty. Did it mean he'd get deployed and disappear into an unknown hell hole for an undetermined amount of time? She wasn't one to name demands as a condition of a relationship, but she didn't feel equipped to raise a child by herself despite the fact she cared deeply for Emma. Trevor wasn't the type of guy who would be happy in a nine-to-five job unless it was military related. Even a military nine to five was a stretch. He was pure Alpha. Life was ride or die.

She was getting ahead of herself. He hadn't mentioned stepping back into a romance. Since the rescue, he'd kept his communication professional and polite.

To gain control of the persistent nervousness about his move out here, she distracted herself by ordering a timed tactical course run through by every trainee. She designed the experience to combine elements of a shooting range with close-quarters battle, challenging participants to demonstrate both marksmanship and sound judgement under simulated combat stress while clearing a building. Participants were evaluated on their firearm skills as well as their decision-making in high-pressure scenarios. As instructor, Kacie controlled the targets with a computer, ensuring each newbie had a unique experience. If any person failed the test, she'd design a specialized course to bring them up to Valor standards. A second failure meant they were out. She had their attention.

"Okay, trainees. I know some of you served and I also know a few will think this is unnecessary because of former military service, but I promise you it's not child's play. Any questions?"

"Yeah. Can I have your phone number?"

"There's always one," she said, shaking her head. "Fall in. Mr. Cocky goes first." She had to admit he was the hottest recruit she'd ever seen with his dark eyes, a rich deep shade of brown, thick, black hair and olive complexion. Never mind the damn near perfect physique on the six-foot frame. She'd review his file later, but she remembered he served as a Navy SEAL and had done three tours. A complete bad ass.

Kacie threw every obstacle in her arsenal at the wise guy but he passed with flying colors. One after another of the trainees ran the course and all but one succeeded. Not bad. At the end of the day, Mr. Cocky approached her and offered to help the failed student through his retrain. She didn't know if he was taking a different approach to obtain her number or if he truly was a team player. She took him up on his offer as a test.

That night she FaceTimed Trevor as agreed to

discuss the move. He commented on how chill she appeared. When she conveyed how she'd spent the day on the course she'd designed, he showed interest and asked if he could try it.

"Of course. I have the perfect battle buddy to team you up with." Mr. Cocky popped into her head.

"Something about your smug smile tells me I'm getting set up but I'll take the challenge." He gave her a thumbs-up. "On a different subject, I brought up the idea of temporarily relocating to Denver with Emma for the equine program and she brightened up at the idea. Her only reluctance was leaving Hazel. But you, plus horses, tipped the scale toward the move."

He said temporarily. All my mental judo for nothing. Trevor wasn't coming here for her. *Time to move on.* Maybe she'd give her number to the new guy. Vince had changed the rules in her contract to no fraternization if on mission or assignment together.

"That's good news. I have pictures of some of the cutest horses and ponies."

"I think the appeal was spending time with you, Kacie." He hesitated. "Will that be possible?"

"Yes. As much as I can. I'll take it from here. Put the little nugget on the call."

"Here's Emma. I'm going downstairs to work."

"Hi, Kacie." As she always did, she held up her bracelet and tapped it with her finger. "I went outside again and this time I wasn't afraid."

"I'm proud of you." She made a heart sign. "I have pictures of the horses you might ride. Want to see?"

"Yes." She tilted her head and glanced down. "I love you. I want you to live with me."

"I love you, too, munchkin." She brushed her

fingers through her hair. *Emma's fragile. I need to give her the perfect response without making promises I can't keep.* "Once you and your daddy move out here, we'll have lots of sleepovers. We can have tea parties and dress up dates, too."

Emma clapped her hands, moving her head left and right. The spark in her blue eyes danced for the first time since the incident.

"I'm sending you the pictures of the horses on your dad's email so you can print them and have copies to look at any time you want. Tell him I'll call him tomorrow."

"I'm here. Never made it downstairs." He leaned over Emma's chair and locked on her with an unflinching gaze. "I wasn't trying to eavesdrop."

"You heard our conversation?" Kacie said.

"All of it."

Chapter Twenty-Seven

Kacie shaded her face with her hand and checked the sky. Bright sun and blue skies were forecast for the next few days. April was a fickle month, and she hoped for Trevor and Emma's sake they arrived in good weather. She remembered an earlier trip to Colorado this same time of year when she left Colorado Springs in light snow and headed up I-25 toward Denver. A blizzard swept in and stranded cars all along the interstate. She crept through near white out conditions as a large X over each exit number and the words, 'exit closed due to blizzard conditions,' displayed on a dynamic message board as she passed. An exit outside the city limits of Denver, still opened, provided an escape route but she spent the next two days locked down in a hotel room.

A day off was hard to obtain with her new job. Training continued with or without her. Her absence meant someone else pulled double duty. The idea bothered her but when she weighed the outcome of giving Emma a sense of security her first day in a new environment or a qualified person stepping in for the short term, the choice was obvious.

Mr. Cocky had accelerated to the top of the class and proven his proficiency in every trial. She reviewed his personnel file and found out he retired from the military as a SEAL Commander after twenty years. He appeared much younger than his actual age of forty-one, an old man by Special Forces standards, but hot enough to pose for a romance book cover or fireman calendar. He stated on his application his goals were to stay active and use his skills to protect others. In the military, the mentality of protection is known as a sheepdog. Someone whose mission is to guard the flock. The more she read, the more she realized she could trust him to cover for her.

"You wanted to see me?" He swaggered up to her in a brown t-shirt fitted tightly across his chest, and desert, camouflage pants. His gun hung low on his hip.

"Yes. I need a favor."

"And I still need your phone number." He handed her a pen and held out his palm for her to write it.

Kacie stuck the pen behind her ear, stood with her arms akimbo and stared him down.

"Okay, okay, what do you need?"

"I'd like you to run the new guys on the course this afternoon."

"As the I/C?"

"Correct. I have confidence in your ability." She tapped the side of her head. "I like the attitude toward the younger guys and ensuring they have high standards."

"Are you calling me old?" He pretended to drag the hilt of a knife from his chest.

His humor charmed her and as much as she tried to resist his appeal, she found it inviting and oddly relaxing. Her mouth didn't go dry around him, or did her chest tighten or her pulse pound. Kacie pulled the pen from her ear and grabbed his hand. She glanced at him with a raised eyebrow and wrote her cell number across his palm.

"Don't share this with anyone. Got it?"

The hum of a car engine approaching jarred her from the SEAL's magnetic personality. She turned toward the sound and eyed Trevor, navigating his Land Cruiser into the circular drive, in front of the main building. Emma was in the seat next to him, waving, and Freya hung out the back window.

She could sense the SEAL's curiosity about the arrival, but the last thing she wanted was an encyclopedia length explanation about their connection.

"Talk later," she stated with finality, and walked toward the car.

"There will definitely be a later," he called after her.

****

"How was your trip?" Kacie said in a casual tone, certain Trevor noticed the SEAL. She reached through his open window and petted Freya who had stepped forward onto the console.

"Long but worth it to be here." He glanced toward the SEAL who jogged by the car and waved. "One of your students?"

"Yep." Kacie focused on Emma, whose eyes were the size of silver dollars. "Hi, Emma. I'm so happy you're here. Are you hungry?"

"I'm thirsty first," she said. "And then hungry."

"We'll have to handle that, young lady." Kacie patted the door frame and stepped back. "Burgers on me." Kacie moved to Emma's window and reached in for a hug. "Do you guys want to freshen up and meet later for burgers?"

"Sure. If it works for your schedule," Trevor said

flatly.

Kacie hated it when Trevor became formal and distant, but she'd give him the benefit of doubt and credit tiredness for his surly mood.

"We rented a house not far from here and paid a company that specializes in home staging to furnish and decorate it."

"Fancy." She smiled and nodded.

"It's on a cul-de-sac and has a seven-foot privacy fence around a large backyard." He glanced at Emma. "For Freya."

"I get it." She winked. "Well, text me the address. I'll get takeout burgers and fries from the best place around and bring them over around six p.m. Sound good?" She directed the question to Emma, who nodded enthusiastically. "One more thing. Tomorrow, we ride."

****

Trevor dipped his French fries in ketchup as he observed Kacie interact with Emma. They were like two peas in a pod. Members of an unknown sisterhood of females who shared their ability to mesmerize men. He thought it had to do with their skill at emotionally connecting to life. A freedom he struggled with both because he was a man and because he was raised to have a British stiff upper lip. *It feels strange not to have you in my life, Kacie.* He wanted to say it out loud.

"Time for you to go to bed," he said to Emma. "We have an early start tomorrow."

"I want Kacie to tuck me in." She peered at him from under her eyelashes.

"I, er…uh…she—" He fumbled with the answer. Kacie wasn't a permanent fixture in their life, and he didn't want Emma hurt.

"I don't mind," Kacie said, interrupting him.

Trevor hugged and kissed Emma. After they disappeared up the stairs, he cleared the table and mentally prepared his speech. Boundaries needed to be established. What role did Kacie play?

"She's asleep." Kacie said in a low voice as she stepped off the bottom stair.

"Can we talk?" Trevor rested his arm on the back of the kitchen chair.

"We should." She sighed and sat across from him. "You first."

"I want to start by saying this was the right move to bring Emma out here. The change of environment alone is a form of therapy. I'm glad you suggested it."

"But?" Kacie tilted her head.

"But was it the right decision for us?" He removed his arm from the back of the chair and folded both arms across his chest.

"I guess that's up to us?" She rubbed her hands down her pants leg. "I owe you an apology for the way I left. I let my emotions control my actions."

"One of the things I love about you is your controlled volatility. You're able to express your emotions without completely losing it. I, on the other hand, am a stewer and a sulker until the lid blows off. That's how I became an expert at damage control." He laughed.

"Well, adulting isn't always easy but we're human and as humans we're organically flawed."

"I like your perspective. It's another thing I admire about you." He relaxed his arms and rubbed his chin. "You're superhuman in how you relate to Emma and

I'm grateful for your friendship. We are friends, correct?"

"I wouldn't go that far," she said waving her index finger back and forth.

"I don't understand?" He rose from his chair, his brows creased in a frown.

"I'm kidding." She threw a napkin at him and laughed. "You think I'd do all this," —she waved her arms in a wide circle— "for people I don't like? I swear. Sometimes you're denser than mud."

In two strides, Trevor was beside her. Grief choked him and blocked his words. He reached for her hands and kissed them before pulling Kacie to her feet. She wrapped her arms around his waist and laid her head on his shoulder. The night he heard Emma and Kacie say they loved each other confirmed his feelings for Kacie. He would love her for the rest of his life.

"You're the best man I know, Trevor Marlowe. I don't know anyone who is a better father than you. Or a better soldier."

"I'm retiring. No more soldiering for the government."

Kacie leaned back and gazed up at Trevor. "What about private soldiering?"

"It occurred to me I might be qualified but the company I'm interested in has this really tough instructor…."

"I heard she's not above having a teacher's pet."

He tilted up her chin and scanned every angle of her face. "I want to drink you in." With his eyes opened he kissed her. She met his gaze and flattened her body against him, deepening the kiss. Without breaking their embrace, he backstepped her to the sofa, easing her down before climbing on top of her. With his fingers on the first button of her blouse, he whispered in her ear describing the pleasure he was going to bring her. She licked her lips when he thought he heard a noise and paused. A giggle erupted from the top of the stairs. Trevor leapt up and ran to the bottom of the staircase. Standing on the top stair, Emma smiled like a cat who had just swallowed a goldfish.

"You like each other again." She clapped her hands together. "It's what I wished for."

Trevor glanced at Kacie, who shrugged and turned her palms outward. "You can handle this one." She chuckled.

"Back to bed young lady," he said trying to sound tough. He sat on the sofa next to Kacie.

"That might have killed the moment," he said it with a smirk.

"There will be more moments, ones even better than this."

"Promise?" He pushed her down on the pillows.

"I promise."

Chapter Twenty-Eight

Kacie arrived early for work. The sooner she handled her tasks, the sooner she could meet Trevor for lunch. They had a lot to discuss. A week had passed since he and Emma moved to Winding Creek. Emma's progress since joining the Mount Up for Wellness program evoked pure joy for Kacie. A small Quarter Horse named Spirit caught Emma's attention on the first day. The Palomino gelding oozed patience and had a quiet disposition. Determined to care for every aspect of the equine, the little redhead insisted on helping with grooming and feeding him as well as riding.

Her first lesson consisted of the counselor leading Spirit around a small corral on a lunge line. The delight on Emma's face showed the kind of relief you experience when your reserve parachute opens after the main one fails. After the fourth lesson, the counselor suggested Emma be dropped off and remain for the entire morning. Kacie must have checked her phone every minute for an urgent message saying Emma's had a meltdown, but the call never came.

With her shoulders thrust back and her back ramrod straight, she sashayed down the main hall of headquarters. For a woman who dropped out of college, against the wishes of her family, and enlisted in the Marines, she'd proven she was worthy of the respect bestowed on her by the staff and fellow veterans. Kacie was a proud Marine.

She strolled past the conference room and glanced in. Blindsided by who she observed in there, she ran headlong into the broad chest of Mr. Cocky.

"Hey, I called, but you ghosted me," he said. "What's up?"

"Shoot. I'm sorry." She pointed in the conference room and said, "That's what's up."

His face flashed with recognition. "I know the British guy or I should say, know *of* him. Is he the reason you vanished?"

"Yes. I owe you an explanation."

"No, you don't. Although I hate losing to the British, well, I just hate losing, but we never got started."

"Friends?"

"I don't have friends but we're good. I'll babysit the newbies for you anytime."

"Thanks." She squeezed his arm before he swaggered away.

She did a double take in the window of the conference room. Trevor and Vince huddled over the computer screen together and discussed whatever they were viewing with apparent interest. As a senior staffer, she took the liberty of tapping on the glass door and entering without waiting for an invitation.

"I'm thinking of hiring this old man. What do you think? Would you recommend him?" Vince said in a joking tone.

"I don't know. How many pushups can he do?" She suppressed a smile.

"Hey, you two. At thirty-nine I'm still in my prime," Trevor grumbled, "and not ready to be put out to pasture."

Freya, who had been resting quietly at his feet, sat up and barked.

"I don't think she's ready to retire either," Kacie said as she rubbed under the dog's chin.

With a wave of his hand Vince indicated Kacie take a seat next to Trevor.

"I need another logistics person," Vince said. "Like yesterday."

"That's right up your alley," she said, with a slight turn in her chair to face Trevor.

"Technically, I'd be your boss." Trevor grimaced, recalling how things ended the last time he was her boss.

"Technically, you never will," she stifled a laugh, "but I'm all about team work so accept the offer if you want the job. I think you'd be fantastic."

"Kacie will still report directly to me. That way the chain of command doesn't get, shall we say, complicated? You two can continue your," Vince hesitated, "dance."

****

Trevor hadn't experienced this much happiness and excitement since Emma was born.

Sitting across from him at a lunch table in her favorite hamburger joint was the most beautiful woman he'd ever seen. In a week, he'd start the best job he'd ever had, a new job as a logistics executive. It was twice the salary paid him in the British military and the challenge was cerebral rather than physical. The best part was he wouldn't be deployed for months but would be local. He could put down roots.

"Move in with me," he said to Kacie.

"I still have months on my lease."

"Your lease allows for subleasing. Are you having second thoughts?"

"No. I'm going to give this relationship everything I've got. I want us to work."

"What's holding you back?"

"I know this is going to sound crazy and like I'm a glass half empty girl but it all seems too perfect. A lot of my current history has been a dumpster fire then all of a sudden it's smooth sailing, like velvet panties. Have we gone soft?"

Trevor put his head on the table and laughed. He attempted to answer Kacie but when he glimpsed her quizzical expression, he lost it again.

"People are staring. What's gotten into you?" She thumped the table with her knuckles.

He finally gained enough composure to spit out the words, "now, I know what I'm getting you for Christmas," he choked back a laugh, "I'll make certain I'm your secret Santa so you unwrap the gift at the company Christmas party." His eyes danced with glee.

She thought for a minute then realized what he'd locked onto. "Oh no you don't. It's called a metaphor. You scoundrel. You will *not* gift me velvet panties, *ever*."

Trevor reached into his pocket and brought out a red velvet box. She gasped.

"Not velvet panties, I promise," Trevor said. He slid from the bench and kneeled on one knee. "You make me laugh and most importantly you've made me whole again. I want to be the best man I can be around you. I will always have your back. Will you marry me?"

"Yes, absolutely, yes." Kacie slid from her seat and knelt beside him while thunderous applause rang throughout the restaurant. She mouthed thank you to the patrons, many of whom she'd seen while dining there with Davy then tilted her head skyward and said thank you again. As Trevor slid the ring on her finger, she viewed the size of the carat and the clarity of the diamond. "You know you didn't need to buy this honker of a ring," she said. "I would have been happy with a simple band."

"There's one more thing." He withdrew a second ring from the red box. This one was made from plastic beads and elastic. "I asked Emma if it would be okay if I married you and she said you have to marry both of us." He slid the second ring on the same finger.

Kacie held her hand out and admired the two rings. "Where is the little sprite?"

"She had an appointment with Spirit today and couldn't be bothered with adult things like proposing marriage."

"I'll go with you to pick her up and tell her I accept in person."

As they drove West toward the highway entrance that would take them to pick up Emma, Trevor reached for Kacie's hand. "I'd given up on ever finding love again until I met you."

"Thanks for choosing me, Trevor, and by the way," —she pointed to the sun dipping low on the horizon— "we are literally driving off into the sunset."

A word about the author…

With close ties to the Navy SEAL community, Connie's mission as a writer is to offer the reader a realistic portrayal of men who transfer their alpha tendencies and athletic prowess into serving a noble cause.

A former English teacher and corporate executive Connie holds a B.A. from East Carolina University. Although she spent many years in the corporate world, her first love has always been writing. She maintains a portfolio of songs, poems and stories she wrote as early as ten. When she isn't creating new plots, Connie enjoys Zumba fitness and claims her best story ideas come to her while dancing the Salsa.

Connie lives near the Gulf Coast of Florida with her German Shepherd Dog and a cat who takes no prisoners.

http://www.connieyharris.com

Thank you for purchasing
this publication of The Wild Rose Press, Inc.

For questions or more information
contact us at
info@thewildrosepress.com.

The Wild Rose Press, Inc.
www.thewildrosepress.com